THE KNIFE EDGE

By

Pat Abercromby

DEDICATION

This story is dedicated to the friends and family of 'Marie'
who refused to leave her side during her long recovery thousands
of miles from home and without whom,
she may not have survived.

CONTENTS

PROLOGUE.. 1

1. Marie, England 3
2. The Aftermath.. 64
3. Fiona, Johannesburg... 70
4. Sally... 87
5. Marie... 127

ABOUT THE AUTHOR 169
BIBLIOGRAPHY...171

ACKNOWLEDGMENTS

Thanks to the brave lady who agreed to share her story of survival after the devastating effects of a burst brain aneurism and gave me the freedom to embellish some (but not much) of her extraordinary struggle to recover her life.

Thanks also to fellow writers and friends who read the first drafts and encouraged me to complete the story.

PROLOGUE

Johannesburg

I am running down a long corridor. In the distance, a door lies almost open. Through the small gap, a glimpse, hazy outlines of people gliding past. I so want to go through - to see for myself what lies beyond. I reach the door. It slams shut. Bereft, lost, confused, sinking to my knees on the coolness of the marble floor.

'Wat is jou naam?'

I open my eyes. I see a generous shape clad in a dark blue tunic. Feel the tightness - painful pressure on my arm. Focus on the pale pinkness of the nails on the three black fingers pressing my wrist.

'Wat is jou naam?' The voice husky, now with a hint of impatience, repeats.

Shiny black cheeks, deep dark, dark, eyes stare at me. The pale insides of the full mouth show, forming a question. What

1

is she saying? Naam? Does she want me to say my name? What is my name? My head hurts. I slip back into the void of unknowing.

'Hello, dear. Can you open your eyes?' The gentleness of a different voice and the warm pressure enclosing my hand make me want to respond, to connect to familiarity, to push my way through the thick fog in my head. Pain. I want this woman to know that I am here, inside. I squeeze her hand. The fog closes round me.

'Well done, you have opened your eyes today. Hi, I'm Fiona. Can you tell me your name? Are you English?' The same soft, Celtic voice, the same warmth from the hand holding mine anchors me. I see her face, blue eyes crinkling in the tanned skin. I feel safer.

'Hello, again. It's Fiona, remember?'

I must be home. I want to see my daughter.

My lips are dry. 'Where is my daughter? Tell her I'm here,' I whisper, desperate now.

Fiona squeezes my hand, leaning closer to my face, smiling. 'Don't worry, dear, your husband is coming to see you in a wee while.'

'No! No! He's not my husband. Keep him away from me!' Agitated, I clutch at Fiona's hand. Darkness enfolds me.

1

Marie, England

He is sitting alone in the front row of the crematorium, shoulders hunched, head bent. Piped music, *Abide With Me,* plays quietly, heralding the imminent arrival of the coffin. I am sitting near the back, with a scattering of his father's old neighbours. My heart tightens with sympathy and nerves as his father's only son turns around and sees me.

I turn to the couple next to me. I remember them from years back. 'Shall we go and join him?' I whisper.

'No thanks. We are here for his dad, not him.'

I feel a bit shocked, seems harsh, I think. Quickly I stand and move forward, slipping into the seat beside him.

He turns to me, tears swimming in his pale eyes, sandy-coloured eyelashes damp and stuck together. 'Thanks Marie,' his voice quivers.

I put a comforting hand on his shoulder as the black-suited pallbearers from the funeral home solemnly and efficiently deposit the coffin on the plinth and back away, heads bowed in professional respect.

It must be at least twenty years since I last saw Guy I am thinking, as the brief committal service proceeds. I had tried to keep up the relationship with Guy's mum and dad. They were Uncle Will and Aunt Joan to my ex, Ricky, who disappeared without trace years ago. They were always so pleased to see me. I was their only connection to gone-Ricky, their nephew, and now in death it would seem, to their son, Guy.

I struggled to remember why Guy had cleared off to Australia with a girlfriend at the tender age of seventeen. I knew that he was a wild kid, always clashing with his father and any other figure of authority that crossed his path. He had been expelled from school for repeatedly smoking and drinking in the school grounds and had been caught shoplifting from Woolworths, outraging and humiliating his parents. Uncle Will was "respectable" and a high ranking Masonic Provincial Grand Almoner. His son's behaviour horrified him.

'Bloody delinquent,' his dad had called Guy. I suspected that Uncle Will had not been too broken-hearted to see Guy leave. Despite being a strict disciplinarian, Uncle Will could not completely control his wayward son. Still, seventeen was very young to let him go and I knew that his mum, Aunt Joan, was really worried about him. She was a sweet-natured gentle soul and for a long time after Guy left, she fretted and grieved for him, her only child.

'Guy is doing ever so well in Australia,' Aunt Joan would tell me when I visited. 'Got his own business, in trees; employs quite a few men and has his own house.' She would proudly produce the photographs of Guy squinting into the camera, face half concealed by a wide-brimmed bush hat (no bobbing corks, mercifully) and faded khaki-coloured shorts, standing in front of a typical Queenslander bungalow with its wrap-around wooden deck. Or chopping wood, bare-chested, wielding a huge axe. The very last time I visited them, the photograph album had a few new disturbing additions. Uncle Will had carved a hunting knife with images of animals etched into the blade and Aboriginal figures into the leather hilt, his hobby and passion. The knife was sent to Guy for his birthday. Not long afterwards, he proudly sent back pictures of himself brandishing the knife triumphantly over the dead body of a large red kangaroo, its neck a gaping red slash, and another one of him using the knife to skin a crocodile.

'He must have thought that would impress me.' Uncle Will pursed his lips and left the room.

Guy's house huddled in the middle of nowhere, surrounded by tall, bluish Eucalyptus and huge, flaky, white-barked Paperbark trees which crowded in, keeping three sides of the house in perpetual, gloomy shade. His block of land remained in its wild state, apart from the area he had cleared in front of the bungalow to park his beaten-up utility van. "Ute" he called it. Storage on wheels for all his tools and tree cutting gear, hidden under a faded, scruffy blue "tarp". It all looked unfriendly and primitive I thought. I could not imagine living in such an isolated setting, not to mention all the creepy-crawlies hiding in the untamed land surrounding his bungalow.

'I just wish he would find a nice Australian girl to marry,' Aunt Joan often said as she sighed heavily and closed the small photograph album with a snap. 'I always hoped to have grandchildren.'

Uncle Will never said much on these occasions, just patting his wife's shoulder, nodding patiently through her oft-repeated narrative.

I could not imagine even a "nice Australian girl" wanting to live outback with Guy and raising children there. Not much chance of ever seeing them even if he did marry, I thought. He only came back once from Australia, still single, for their silver wedding anniversary.

After Aunt Joan died, still longing for her son and unborn grandchildren, Uncle Will moved away from Surrey to a small bungalow on the coast. I felt guilty that I had stopped visiting him, but honestly, I was so busy juggling my life, raising my daughter on my own, working full-time to pay the bills and caring for my widowed mother. Mum suffered from crippling arthritis for years and was totally dependent on Dad for everything. When he died suddenly from a burst aneurism in his heart, I took over his job of caring for her. I was heartbroken at the time but there was no time to mourn properly for him. Mum needed immediate support. I had no choice.

I did occasionally phone Uncle Will and always sent him a Christmas card with the latest photo of Sally, my daughter. Pretty, talented Sally, whizzing back and forth to audition for parts in musicals and cabarets, after she graduated with a Diploma in Performing Arts. She took after her dad, Ricky, the extrovert DJ, the compulsive entertainer. I experienced waves of mixed emotions; pride and sadness and some anxiety as my successful daughter was drawn deeper into the entertainment world. I fervently hoped that Sally would avoid the temptations that had finished her dad's career.

It had been a guilty shock for me to get an unexpected call from Guy, all the way from Australia.

'Marie, it's Guy, you know, Will's son.' His accent was very obviously Australian although his voice kept cracking up. 'Marie, Dad died this morning, 5am your time. I didn't know who else to call.'

'Oh, I am so sorry, Guy, I didn't know he was ill. I haven't been to see him for a while.'

'I just spoke to him two days ago, he was planning a trip out to visit me. He was in good spirits, excited about travelling again after Mum… you know…' his voice faltered.

I bit my lip, trying to find the right words for this newly-orphaned grown-up man. A man I barely remembered. I had met Guy just a couple of times at family gatherings before he went to live in Australia and once a few years later when he came back for his parents' wedding anniversary. Ricky was a few years older than Guy. It was obvious to me and everyone else who saw them, that the cousins did not get on. Ricky said Guy was a waste of space, a sponger, living at home with his mum and dad and never bothering to look for a job after he was expelled from school. They were poles apart in personality, but uncannily similar in their shared dislike of conventional rules.

He and Ricky nearly came to blows at that party. Guy was in his early twenties then and had filled out into a sturdy, strong, outdoor type, already tanned and prematurely lined from exposure to the scorching sunlight of Queensland. However, I noticed that Uncle Will was still finding fault with him. Complaining that he was drinking too much, grumbling that it was time he "settled down" like Ricky.

Ricky had a lot of respect for Uncle Will, his only male relative. He told me he never knew his own dad who ran off when he was a baby. He was an only child, like his cousin Guy; raised in a rough part of east London by his mother and grandmother. No spoiling for him, they were a tough pair. His grandmother was harder on him than his mother and he spent as much time out of the house as he could to avoid her harsh punishments. Early on in his life, he had to gain street cred in his neighbourhood to survive. Unlike Guy, he never resorted to petty crime, but got along by being a clown and joking his way out of trouble. When he was twelve his mum moved to East Sussex, but Ricky hated living so far away from London. As soon as he could, at sixteen, he left home and moved back to London. To his roots. He admitted to me that he hardly ever bothered visiting his mum after that. Uncle Will had tried to be a surrogate father-figure to Ricky, but as they had by then moved to Surrey, Ricky rarely visited until he married me. Family life was important to me and I encouraged Ricky to visit his mum in Sussex and aunt and uncle in Surrey as often as we could.

I was very aware that Uncle Will much preferred Ricky over his own son. He loved listening to Ricky's funny stories. That day, he had been laughing uproariously. Ricky, as usual, sharing a joke as they stood leaning companionably on the free bar in the British Legion Hall that had been hired for the party. I was sitting talking with Aunt Joan. My chair was facing the bar. I couldn't help noticing Guy, excluded, glaring at his dad and Ricky, and wishing that Uncle Will didn't make it so obvious that he preferred Ricky's company. Another man joined them at the bar, attracted by the laughter, no doubt. Ricky excused himself and came over to me and Aunt Joan. He bent over me and gave me a full-on, beer-flavoured kiss.

'Just going outside for a fag, love. Coming?'

We were still in the honeymoon phase of our marriage, before Sally, our daughter, was born. I couldn't help it, I was still infatuated with him then. He had the charisma of a professional performer. He leant over to embrace Aunt Joan who blushed and kissed his cheek.

'Do you mind if I borrow my beautiful wife, Aunt Joan? I want to show her off to some of your friends.'

Aunt Joan quickly said, 'Of course, of course, you lucky boy, I have been keeping Marie to myself for far too long.'

Ricky pulled me to my feet, wrapping his arm possessively round my waist and led me towards the door. 'You look gorgeous in that blue dress, darling. Let's find somewhere private for a quick snog.' He nibbled playfully at my neck and I felt my insides doing their usual flip-flop as they always did every time he touched me.

I am not quite sure exactly how it happened but remembered that Guy had barged into Ricky almost causing me and Ricky, so closely entwined, to lose our balance.

'Oi! Watch where you're going mate. You nearly knocked us over!'

I thought I heard Guy mutter, 'Pommy bastard,' as he continued walking out through the door.

I was left standing alone as Ricky made a lunge for Guy, spun him round and grabbed the front of his shirt.

'What did you call me?' They were almost nose to nose. I was afraid that Ricky would throw a punch. He could lose his temper in a flash.

Fortunately, Uncle Will appeared and yelled at them. 'Break it up, you two! Show some respect. This is not the time or place for a fight.'

The two men stepped back, still glaring at one another, but Uncle Will was not to be messed with. Guy disappeared around the corner of the building and Ricky smiled apologetically at his uncle as he sauntered casually back to me. I hate confrontation and felt cross with Ricky, but as usual, he won me round with his insouciant charm.

'Sorry about that, babe, but Guy is such a dick. Just as well he lives in Australia,' he said as he pulled me closely into his side and led me outside.

That was the last time Ricky and I had seen Guy

after he returned to his life in Australia.

*

'So sorry, Guy,' I had repeated helplessly. 'You must have been so shocked. Are you coming home?' Thinking rapidly, God I hope so, there are no other relatives alive to arrange a funeral as far as I know. Ricky disappeared years ago.

'Yes, of course, I am leaving in a few hours to catch a flight south to Brisbane and then on to Gatwick. I will go straight to Dad's house and start arranging his funeral. There's nobody else now.' Once again, his voice broke.

'Please let me know if I can do anything to help you, Guy.'

'Thanks, Marie, I'll let you know about the funeral. Will you come?'

'Yes, of course I will Guy. Ricky and I split up a few years ago, I don't have an address for him, he might be in Sweden, but I don't know where. Sorry.'

'Don't be sorry, Marie, I never thought he was the right person for you. You deserved better.'

I signed off feeling puzzled, what did he mean by that? I had hardly ever spoken more than a few words to him the couple of times I had met him all those years ago. He was partly right though, life with Ricky had been a rollercoaster ride from the moment I met him…

*

Being 19 in the late '70s, the music scene was an exhilarating time for me. I was happy living at home, loved club music and had a big circle of friends. Our main form of entertainment was dancing at nightclubs to Jazz-Funk, House and Soul music. I would go out on dates with a few of the club regulars, but I wasn't looking for a serious relationship, it was all about the music and dancing and just having fun with the young guys who shared my taste in club music. My male colleagues in the bank were older, serious, conventional types, there was nobody there I wanted to date. I preferred the guys at the club, nearly always sporting their uniform of black t-shirts, short leather jackets and baggy jeans which would slip over their skinny backsides, revealing a sliver of split porcelain flesh as their moves on the dance floor grew wilder.

I had noticed the DJ, his name was Ricky, but he had a big following of girl fans who would always be gyrating in front of him, hoping to be noticed. He had long dark curly hair, almost as long and dark as my own, a full generous mouth and a slight curve on the

14

bridge of his nose which gave him a wild, gypsy look. Made me shiver a little. But there was no way I would be joining the pack of girls vying for his attention. I had plenty of my own admirers then.

One night, an attractive lad who had been dancing near me all night, started chatting just as I was leaving. He was nice, lovely accent, said his name was Noah and lived in Sweden. He said he was going back to Sweden the following evening, but could we meet up for lunch? I quickly gave him my phone number and hurried off to catch a lift with my friends who were leaving. The next day I was surprised and pleased, to get a call from him and we arranged to meet near my bank in London. I was having dinner with my brother that evening so had dressed smartly in a blue suit and was wearing my killer high heels. My brother was always a sharp dresser, so I did not want to show him up when he took me to his favourite Italian bistro not far from where I worked.

Noah came rushing up to me as I waited for him outside my bank. I was disappointed, he was dressed in scruffy jeans and a stained t-shirt.

'Hi, Marie, I am so sorry to turn up dressed like this, but I was helping a friend move some stuff and I did not want to be late meeting you. You look gorgeous by the way.' He leaned in and kissed my cheek.

'Oh, don't worry, Noah, we can just grab a coffee somewhere nearby.' Pity, I thought to myself, he is quite nice, but he is leaving for Sweden tonight, probably never see him again anyway.

'Please, Marie, I want to take you to lunch, let's get a cab back to my place so that I can change my clothes.' He was hailing a cab as he spoke, so I took a leap of faith and went along with him.

He made me a cup of tea while he showered and changed. I was quite relaxed waiting for him to emerge and was now looking forward to having lunch with him. He was very charming and had made me laugh during our taxi ride to his flat in Hornsey, North London.

I was looking out of the window at the matching block of grey-clad flats opposite when the front door opened with a bang. A man walked past me without saying a word, went straight into the kitchen, made himself a cup of tea, marched back out and slumped down heavily on an armchair opposite me.

'Who are you?' he grumbled moodily without bothering to make eye contact.

I thought he looked vaguely familiar but could not place him. He was wearing a black baseball cap pulled low on his forehead and was staring into his mug of tea. He was a real grump, I thought, and rude with it. I decided to be offhand back with him.

'I'm waiting for Noah, he's getting changed.'

'Oh, Noah's here is he?'

'Well, I didn't just break in and make myself a cup of tea!' I said sarcastically, thinking what a curmudgeon he was. He must be Noah's flatmate. Fortunately, Noah reappeared and we left without me exchanging any more words with the grump. Noah and I enjoyed our short time together that day, but both of us accepted that a long-distance relationship would not work when he returned to live and work in Sweden, although he did promise to contact me any time he came back to London.

A week later I was back at my favourite club, dancing with my friends when the DJ announced:

'OK, time to slow it down people.' This next track is dedicated to the beautiful girl in the blue top with the hot dance moves.' Ricky the DJ grinned straight at me across the sea of dancers, now all swivelling their heads to see who he meant. I was mortified and tried to get off the dance floor as quickly as possible, but Ricky grabbed my hand and pulled me over to a spot close to the DJ's box. *Lovin You* by Minnie Ripperton was playing at full volume. He pulled me into his arms and we swayed together for a few bars of the song.

'You're the girl that was in my flat last week,' he said staring intently into my face.

'Oh, so you were the rude grump. I didn't know it was your flat, or that it was you.'

Up close, he was incredibly attractive in his white, open-necked shirt, sleeves rolled up to his elbows, revealing toned forearms covered in fine black hairs. I could feel the heat rising from my toes to my face as he pulled me closer. The hardness of his body against mine was intoxicating.

'I'm sorry I was in a foul mood that day. My girlfriend dumped me two months ago and Noah was helping me to move the last of her stuff out. She gave me a lot of grief about some CDs and clothes she said were missing. Accused me of selling them! Imagine!'

'It's OK. Sorry to hear that. I can understand why you were upset.'

He grinned at me. 'I'm feeling better by the minute just looking at you. I'll take you out to dinner to make amends for being rude. I'm not working tomorrow. Meet me at 7pm?'

I was flattered and surprised, but he was so

confident and those big brown eyes of his were irresistible. I realized I was smiling and nodding idiotically in agreement. 'All right, it's a date.'

'Wear that blue top again, it shows up the colour of your eyes.'

We arranged a place to meet in the West End and it was only after he had hurried back to his deck that I realized he hadn't asked me my name.

I did wear my blue top again on that first date. He took me to a small Italian restaurant on the Cromwell Road. We ate *tagliatelle al forno*, followed by *tiramisu* and drank a large carafe of the house red wine between us. I don't remember much about that conversation, Ricky did most of the talking, his brown eyes never leaving my face. I was mesmerized by him. He was very funny and we found so much to laugh about as he shared stories about his early disastrous gigs when he was learning to be a DJ. As we walked hand in hand along the Cromwell Road, he burst into a loud and very tunefully accurate rendition of *Maria* from *West Side Story*.

I think I was already in love with him after that first night and before long we were spending every available moment together. On his days off he would come and meet me for lunch and then wait around for me to finish work at five, so we could spend a long evening together.

I always went to his club on Friday nights with my friends and quite enjoyed the envious looks I got from some of his followers when he would call me back to dance near him in front of the DJ box. Not that that would stop some of the more determined girls who would push past me to fling their arms round his neck and beg for their song request to be played. He would just laugh and wink at me. I felt quite proud of him and his popularity. It never occurred to me at the time that his demands for my constant presence in his orbit were anything other than touching. I felt very cherished by him.

'They wouldn't give me a second look if I wasn't the DJ,' he would reassure me; and to be fair, it was not other women who were the biggest threat to our relationship as I was yet to find out.

These were heady days for both of us in our loved-up bubble, so when he proposed six months later, after a romantic dinner in a restaurant in Camden Passage to celebrate my 21st birthday, I did not hesitate to accept. He even went down on his knees and of course everyone in the restaurant was agog with interest and broke into spontaneous applause when he slipped the ring onto my finger. It was a beautiful sapphire set in a circle of diamonds and it fitted perfectly. He raised my hand to his lips as he stood up beside me. I knew blue was his favourite colour. It had become mine too. I was perfectly happy that he had chosen my engagement ring without me being involved. A pattern of his that continued during our marriage…

'Marie, I can't wait to marry you. If I give you six months until September 6th, that is a good time for me to book leave for our honeymoon, can we arrange the wedding for that date?'

I was thrilled and to be honest, a little overwhelmed at how quickly we had reached this point and stunned at the prospect of arranging a wedding so quickly. I need not have worried. As soon as we told all our friends and my family, Ricky only had his mum and aunt and uncle on his side, plus of course all his mates in the music industry, they all immediately sprang into action to make all the arrangements. All I had to do was to choose my wedding dress.

My family loved Ricky from the first time he met them all. He fitted in so well and was always the life and soul of the party. Considering he barely bothered with his own relatives, I was surprised at how quickly he embraced my own large family. I was born into a large Catholic family of mixed Portuguese and Spanish settlers in Guyana, South America. I barely remember my life there as we left when I was three, after the troubles and rioting started, but I do recall playing with my brothers and cousins in the shade under our wooden house which was raised on stilts. All my life I have been surrounded by loving relatives who all soon followed us to live in England. Organising a wedding for me in six months was just what they were born to do. One uncle, who was a chef, made the wedding cake, my aunts, cousins and mum organised the venue, flowers, guest list, invitations-everything was taken care of. My friends arranged my hen night and my youngest brother, a chauffeur, drove me and my dad to the church. I was blessed to be so cared for by my great family and now to be married to my exciting, funny and unconventional Ricky who loved visiting my family as much as I did.

The only song we ever considered to be "ours" was "The Girl from Ipanema", the Brazilian bossa nova jazz tune from the 1960s! Only because every bar we visited during our first holiday together in Spain would play the song at some stage during the evening. We always had a giggle whenever the song was played because Ricky always changed the words and sang, '*SHORT and tanned and young and lovely, the girl from Ipanema goes walking'*. Even now, after all this time, my heart flips a little when I hear that song. How closely he held me as we danced to the bossa nova rhythm until he would swing me out and twirl me back into his arms. I would be breathless and laughing as I followed his crazy moves.

As soon as we were married, Ricky persuaded me to give up my day job, otherwise we would rarely have had any time together as Ricky worked nights at the clubs. I soon found out that he was wild and impulsive all the time. It was like living in a perpetual whirlwind of spontaneous daytime adventures. He would whisk me off to the coast for the day, just because the sun was shining through our thin bedroom window curtains and woke us up earlier than usual.

'C'mon sweetheart, let's take a drive to Brighton and eat fish and chips on the front in the fresh air. We can be back in time for my gig tonight.'

Ricky didn't drive then, he had always lived and worked in London, so did not see the need for a car. We had bought our first house in Addington, a small two up two down ex-council house on a big residential estate, all we could afford at the time as we were living on Ricky's earnings. I loved making the small rooms homely and comfortable for us, although Ricky commandeered the second bedroom to store his vast record collection. Just as well I was practical and tidy, Ricky was hopeless at anything domestic, but I think he relished having me to organise him. I often went to his gigs with him and observed with pride, how well he worked the crowds, he was such a showman, a natural performer.

Ricky had a good relationship with several of the major record companies in the seventies and eighties. They put him on their mailing lists to receive free "white label 12-inch copies" of new music to be played on the club circuit before being put out for general release to the public. In return, mailing list jocks had to provide valuable feedback on clubbers' reactions to the new music and bands. Our postman always complained about the weight and amount of records in his mailbag for deliveries to our house. Most days, hazardous, trip-making piles of records would arrive and be left outside the front door. Each day Ricky would listen to the new music the record companies had sent and know instantly if it would be a "floor filler" and a big selling club anthem or just another "one for the garbage".

He was in great demand and playing at some of London's most prestigious nightclubs including: The Empire, Leicester Square, Camden Palace, Limelight just off Shaftesbury Avenue and my favourite, Madame JoJo's in Soho. I liked it there as there was always a cabaret featuring a variety of different acts, it made for an entertaining evening out for me. As well as being Ricky's driver I was his reluctant dresser and hairstylist. I always made sure he stood out from the crowd, no point in looking like every other clubber at the venue. Sometimes he needed to wear a dress shirt if the gig was a posh affair.

With me helping him to be organised and because of his increasing popularity in the nightclub circuit, we decided to start up an entertainment agency. It was quite easy as Ricky had so many contacts with other DJs, bands and singers. Word soon spread that he was the go-to guy when clients wanted a specific type of entertainment for private parties or events. Ricky was so popular, that many of his more well-heeled clients insisted on booking him to personally DJ at their event, which, of course, great for business as they paid generously for him to appear. Sometimes he would cover three events in an evening and come home at dawn exhausted...

One morning the birds' dawn chorus woke me up

before Ricky made it upstairs and fell into bed beside me, exhausted and still smelling of stale cigarette smoke. Normally that did not bother me too much, I was so used to it, but this morning the smell turned my stomach and I had to get up and rush into the bathroom to vomit spectacularly.

This was a game-changer for us. Ricky was thrilled that he was going to become a father.

'You realise that I soon won't be able to drive you to the nightclubs, my love. I couldn't cope with the late nights and the smells.' I had to warn Ricky. The smell of cigarettes, alcohol, sweat and the mixed bouquets of expensive perfumes would instantly make me feel sick. I assumed that feeling would pass after the first few months, but I was queasy for the entire pregnancy, and at six months I had doubled my girth. I was huge, and towards the end could only waddle along for a few steps before I had to have a rest. Sally, our daughter, took a long, long time trying to fight her way out of my body and in the end, exhausted and in danger of losing the baby, I had to have an emergency C-section.

'Oh, she is beautiful, Marie! Look, she is just a mini me.' Ricky had tears in his eyes as he cradled his daughter with her mop of black hair and her intense milky brown eyes searching his face with the puzzled concentration of the newborn.

I was traumatised and in pain. 'Yes, she is beautiful and amazing Ricky, but I'm telling you now, once was enough. I can never go through that again.' I meant it too.

Ricky did finally get his driving licence, but he was always over the alcohol limit when he left the nightclubs and was spending a fortune on taxis to bring him home in the early hours to our new family house in Buckinghamshire. The entertainment agency was doing well and I was still able to manage to help him with arranging the bookings in between feeding and looking after the baby. To avoid haemorrhaging so much money on taxis, Ricky employed a 'roadie' called Whizz, one of his regulars from the nightclub scene, who would pick him up and take him and his equipment to his gigs. Sometimes he would have to go to someone's estate in Surrey or other home county to DJ at a special occasion, usually an 18th or 21st birthday party for some privileged young person with their equally wealthy set of friends. Whizz was a wild man, erratic and full of manic energy at times. I did not fully trust him and hated it when Ricky let him stay with us "just overnight" which often extended into a week or more. I had less control over

Ricky's activities now and began to suspect that he might be using drugs to keep him awake or possibly to help him sleep. He was always twitchy and restless in bed after the gigs.

'OK Marie, I admit that I have to take sleeping pills now. It's hard to sleep after a long night at the clubs and Sally's crying keeps me awake, but don't worry, I'm not addicted to any drug. Trust me on that.'

So, I did, until one morning when curious Sally was about three and into everything, she found a packet of white powder on the floor in the bathroom. I was furious and stomped into our bedroom to challenge him. He was sprawled on the bed, out cold, and I couldn't wake him up. He just groaned and turned away. It was pointless, I would have to let him sleep it off and yell at him when he woke up. But what to do? I adored him, so did Sally. I knew he would cajole and charm me and promise that he could give it all up any time - and I would believe him, because I wanted to, needed to. Life without Ricky was unthinkable.

By the early eighties, the club scene ramped up massively and Ricky of course was right in the thick of it all, loving every minute. He was working with a new wave of club DJs who called themselves the

"Soul Funk Mafia". They played soul and jazz funk mixes for clubbers at gigs, soul weekenders and all-nighters, which sprang up all over the country playing to the huge following of devotees to the music or their favourite DJ. He was spending less and less time with me and Sally by then as he was so exhausted after being up all night, sometimes all weekend, that he would be a wreck for two or three days afterwards. But Ricky was proud to be working with DJ royalty (as they were known) and his own devoted club fans grew steadily in number and followed him from gig to gig, often in old, beaten-up VW camper vans. The pace of life for all of them on this new and exciting scene was frenetic, and my involvement with that side of Ricky's work was slipping out of my control.

When Sally started school and Ricky was sleeping off for longer and longer, the effects of the drugs that he still wasn't addicted to, I was bored witless with staying at home while Ricky slept all morning. I took a part-time job in a bank and felt easier having an outlet from home and frankly, from Ricky, who was either semi-comatose or manically energetic, particularly when his roadie, Whizz, and sometimes other hangers-on were sleeping off their hangovers in our lounge. Ricky would sometimes collect Sally from school and of course, soon became a huge hit with all the parents and children at the school gate. He could not stop himself entertaining everybody, they all loved him. But he was crazy and impulsive at home and totally impractical. One day, I came home after a full day at work, having left Ricky in charge of Sally. He managed to get out of bed early and promised to get her to school on time. At 4pm when I came through the door, Sally was still in her pyjamas with damp patches on the knee.

'Why is Sally still in her pyjamas? Did you not take her to school?' I was beyond exasperation.

'Well, we decided to go to the seaside. Didn't we, Sally? Far too nice a day to go to school. We went to Brighton and had ice cream, didn't we, darling?'

'You took her to Brighton in her PYJAMAS! You're mad and irresponsible!' I was yelling.

'Don't be cross with Daddy, we had fun, Mummy. What does irri-irripossible mean?'

'You explain that to your daughter, Ricky, I am going to make dinner. I don't suppose she has had anything substantial to eat either.' And I marched out of the room, irritated and frustrated.

Inevitably, Ricky became more addicted to cocaine and alcohol. Increasingly, he was drunk or spaced out, even during the day. The rave scene had just kicked off and Ricky got heavily involved in that too. The all-night dance parties with the techno music and hypnotic laser lights, not to mention the cocaine he took to keep going, must have been affecting his brain, already under stress from years of alcohol and drug abuse. His behaviour was now mostly unpredictable and he began suffering from paranoia and panic attacks. Business mail was left unopened, flung into the back of a drawer and important phone calls were left unanswered. I tried to fire-fight the chaos for him as much as I could, but eventually, we were floundering. What if he picked up Sally from school and had an accident or took her on an impulse to some sleazy part of London to buy his cocaine? He had been in rehab once but checked himself out. He was out of the loop of acting as DJ at the celebrity gigs where he would be handed packets of cocaine as a bonus.

Sally was so influenced by Ricky, she too wanted to be an entertainer and already had her career mapped out in her mind. I was determined to protect Sally from Ricky's drug abuse. I gave him an ultimatum, go to rehab, get clean, otherwise we are finished. I think that threat must have scared him because he went into rehab again. I took Sally to the Chelsea clinic a week later to visit Ricky and encourage him. Sally was missing her dad. He had checked out. I was in total shock. Ricky knew that checking out this time would lose him his marriage, but the lure of his mistress, cocaine, was more powerful.

He went to live with his mother until our divorce was finalized, then, one day, without any warning, he left his mother's house, leaving all he possessed behind and never came back. Disappeared without a trace. Sally was devastated at first, couldn't believe that her beloved dad had just deserted her. Then the rage against him set in. How could he do that to her? They had such a special relationship, surely he would not betray her by leaving? But he had. Two years went by before he finally made contact, at first sending Sally a card for her eighteenth without a return address, but postmarked Sweden. Eventually he included a return address with a letter, saying he was living with a Swedish woman with three children of her own! Sally took that news very badly, but by then she was in the middle of her college course and stopped talking about her dad.

Ricky had never managed to give us any financial support after he became too addicted to cope with work and I soon discovered that our savings account had been cleared out, presumably most of the money disappearing up his nose. I had a full-time job by then but had to take on evening work to pay the bills. I looked after the London homes of a couple of minor celebrities. At least Ricky's contacts in the entertainment world had proved useful.

Then Dad died unexpectedly from a burst aneurysm in his heart, and almost overnight, I had to become my mother's carer. Mum had bad arthritis and relied heavily on Dad for everything. He paid all their bills and did all the shopping and cooking for them. Before he died, Mum was in a wheelchair and had become heavily dependent. Most weekends, I would go to Mum to shop, clean and cook for her. It was exhausting, and honestly, I hardly had time to feel lonely, except occasionally I would remember Ricky and the constant buzz of excitement around him and the passion that we shared, which was probably why I slipped into an unlikely relationship with Mark, the city high flyer and so much younger than me.

I was introduced to him one rare night out when I had drinks with some friends from work and he made it clear that he was very attracted to me and had no problem with our age difference. I couldn't help being flattered by that. He had his own place and we would get together when we had time. I could never work out why he seemed so keen on me, perhaps because I made no demands on him, and just enjoyed our limited time together. He was a bit of light relief for me in an otherwise exhaustingly busy life. After three years of this undemanding routine with Mark, his bank transferred him to their Manchester branch.

'I want you to come and live with me in Manchester, Marie, we get on so well, it will work. Maybe we could even start a family?'

I was shocked to hear him say this. A family? No way!

'No, Mark, I can't move to Manchester with you. I need to be in the South East for Mum, and Sally is too young still to leave her to fend for herself.' But the real deal-breaker for me, of course, was being asked to consider another pregnancy. I had not forgotten the horrors of delivering Sally. Plus, I was forty and Sally was almost grown up. There was no way I was prepared to go through all that again and to be truthful, Mark was sweet, but he wasn't Ricky. I could never completely forget my feelings for Ricky however traumatic the last few years of living with him had been before we broke up. No one compared.

'I'm sorry, Mark, I just couldn't go through with another pregnancy at my age. You should find a younger woman to start a family with,' I added as gently as I could.

Eventually Mark stopped trying to persuade me and, sadly, we decided to split up. I quickly slipped back into my routine with my full-time work and looking after Mum and Sally. It was a relief in a way not to have to fit in time for Mark as well. Looking for another relationship was the last thing on my mind.

*

Soon after his dad's funeral, Guy had to fly back to his business in Australia.

'Marie, I have to go back for a while to make sure my blokes are working properly. But when I come back, I want to pack up Dad's house and sell it as quickly as possible. I can't stay away from my business for too long. Will you help me please? I am not sure how to go about things in this country.'

I pulled a face at the phone. I could do without this, I was run off my feet as it was with my jobs, looking after Mum and supporting Sally. 'Oh, all right, Guy, but I can only come down one or two weekends. You should put the house on the market now before you leave. Get cleaners to come in and clean and tidy it for you and when you come back, I will help you to pack it up. That shouldn't take too long.'

It was a nightmare. Guy would break down in tears every time he pulled out a drawer and found memorabilia of his father's. His dad's collection of knives, carved with elaborate designs into the handles, family photographs of the three of them, his mum and dad on a caravan holiday on the Isle of Wight when Guy was a boy, a silver cigarette lighter engraved with his dad's initials W.R., even his dad's faded striped pyjamas neatly folded in his chest of drawers. The sight of all of them reduced Guy to paroxysms of grief and I, packing suspended, had to spend ages handling his sorrow, trying to offer him some comfort - aware that the precious weekend time I had reluctantly given up, was ticking away. I did feel quite sorry for him but found his constant outpourings of grief hard to handle, and slightly repelling. I just wished he would keep his emotions in check.

It took three of my weekends to get the contents of the seaside bungalow packed up. Guy was shipping some boxes of his dad's things back to Australia and the Salvation Army came for the rest. It was such a relief when finally, I had done as much as I could for him at the bungalow. It sold quickly. West Wittering was a perfect area for retiring downsizers. He had a few ends to tie up before completing the sale and returning to Australia. We said goodbye and I left him with a sigh of relief at a B&B to finalise the completion of the sale before he flew back home to his single life and his business "in trees". Gratefully, I returned home to resume my familiar, busy routine, glad to be free of his oppressive and draining emotional outbursts.

He phoned me every day to give unwanted updates on how the sale was progressing; contracts had been exchanged and a completion date was being discussed. He was remarkably cheerful. Then.

'Marie, I have a favour to ask you.'

I squeezed my eyes shut trying not to let him sense my irritation. What would it be now? My hand was hurting. I was holding the phone too tightly. 'OK, what is it?' Trying to sound bright.

'My buyers can't complete for another three weeks, but there is nothing for me to do down here and it's not worth flying back to Oz for such a short time.' He paused. 'Any chance I could come and stay with you for three weeks? I would really appreciate it.'

I closed my eyes in exasperation, oh please no. But didn't feel I could refuse. It was only for three weeks, I could surely handle that? I did have a spare room and anyway I would be out at work all day and visiting Mum at the weekends. Guy would just have to see to himself.

I still had to take a deep breath before answering.

'Yes, that's fine, Guy. I have a spare room you can have. It's only got a futon, but it's quite comfortable, especially if it is just for three weeks.'

Sally had just left home to be part of the entertainment team on a cruise liner, which just as well. I had a feeling my feisty daughter would find Guy a bit too hard going. Sally knew that Ricky had hated Guy and although she had not actually met him, she simply reflected Ricky's opinion and would have labelled Guy "anal".

I was pleasantly surprised at the change in him. The over-emotional, needy behaviour he had displayed at the bungalow, had been replaced by a calm, controlled serenity. Maybe he had finally come to terms with the death of his father? When I tried to analyse it, I decided that probably he had been particularly upset, as his father had been planning an imminent trip out to Australia. After all, he had not seen his dad for twenty years. To have that opportunity snatched away must have been particularly upsetting. So, I relaxed and left for work as usual the next day, confident that this new, calmer Guy would be able to cope on his own.

I came home that evening, exhausted as usual, to the smell of cooking. The kitchen was tidy and the table set for two. Marvellous!

'My goodness, thank you, Guy. What a surprise. I was not expecting you to cook for me too.'

Guy smiled, pleased. 'No worries, Marie. It is the least I can do. I sorted out the laundry too.'

We had a pleasant conversation about some of the interesting countries he had visited over the years, no tears or emotional outbursts. Such a relief. He had made a shepherd's pie and side salad. Surprisingly good. When I went up to my bedroom later, sure enough, a neat pile of folded laundry was sitting on the end of the bed. I wasn't too comfortable about him processing the underwear that I had left in the laundry basket under the towels, but it had been so good to come home to a cooked meal and a tidy house, that I decided not to make any comment about him handling my bras and knickers, and just enjoy the novelty of someone else taking care of things for a change. The same pattern of Guy cooking and cleaning the house for me continued and soon I was looking forward to coming home after work to a hot meal and some pleasant company in the evenings.

Inevitably he had a few irritating habits. My mail was always separated into neat piles, one of junk mail and the other pile addressed to me "in order of importance". At first, he would stand too close to me as I opened my letters, questioning me about their contents. He wanted to know why my letters were addressed to Mrs and not Miss, asking if I was actually divorced from Ricky. He told me I should check my phone bill to make sure I was not being overcharged as those companies were all out to "rip you off". I thought he was being ridiculous and told him quite sharply that I would deal with my own business myself thank you. However, I did leave the opened mail in the kitchen which I later wondered if he may have checked to see who I was calling.

He had been staying with me for a few days and when I came back from work, he had rearranged the furniture in my lounge. He moved my comfy armchair and footstool that I liked to sit in to watch television, over to the side and replaced it with my two-seater sofa. This meant that if I wanted to be square-on to the screen, I would have to squeeze in beside him on the sofa. It felt too claustrophobic. He was a big fellow and there wasn't enough room for me to curl my feet under, so I moved the sofa and my armchair until they shared the prime spot in front of the television.

'You shouldn't be pushing furniture around by yourself, Marie. Sheilas like you are not strong enough, you could hurt your back.' He smiled disarmingly.

I just laughed. 'You're like Crocodile Dundee, Guy, thinking all women are helpless. Don't forget I have had to manage on my own for years since Ricky...' I tailed off, seeing Guy's lips setting into a hard line at the mention of Ricky's name. 'Anyway,' I continued, 'they don't call me Mighty Mouse for nothing,' and flexed my firm biceps at him.

'Why do you have to go to your mother's again today? You went yesterday, surely that's enough for one weekend?'

I was surprised and irritated by Guy's presumption. He had sounded annoyed, as if he had the right to interfere in my commitment to my mother. Maybe he was just expressing concern for me I reasoned. I'd had a particularly challenging week at work with review meetings with my line manager - always a bit nerve-wracking - and I had been tired and gone to bed early, leaving Guy to watch television on his own most evenings that week. Feeling pressured, I invited him to come with me to Mum's that Sunday. Out of loyalty to Ricky I suppose, I had not told any of the family, including Sally, that Guy was staying at my house. They all knew that Ricky and Guy disliked one another and because all my relatives had loved Ricky, I felt slightly guilty to be entertaining Guy. Mum was not as sharp as she had been, I did wonder if she was developing some sort of dementia and I was not sure how she would react to Guy.

He had been charming to Mum, although I realised that she was struggling to understand what he was saying. His strong Australian accent and expressions like "fair dinkum" left Mum slightly bemused, but she smiled benignly at him as he kissed her cheek when we left. I got the impression that she was not totally clear who he was. Still, he would be gone very soon and she would have forgotten all about him before my next visit, almost guaranteed.

*

The following day, Guy took a phone call from his solicitor. His buyers were asking for an extension of another week until their completion date. He was in the hallway and I could hear him grumbling at his solicitor about this being 'unacceptable.' He came back into the kitchen holding the phone in his hand to tell me what had been said.

'Gee, I'm sorry, Marie. Is it OK with you if I stay on here for another week?'

Well, who wouldn't be OK with another week of

being spoiled? I was quite enjoying his company, although I wouldn't be too sorry when it was time for him to leave finally. But he was an extremely helpful house guest. A cooked dinner waiting for me every night was magic. Although his constant habit of rearranging my furniture and kitchen cupboards and trying to organize me was irritating at times. I would be glad to get my home back to its normal and slightly chaotic state, after he left.

It was only for one more week. 'Yes of course, Guy. No worries!' I tried out my best Australian accent.

When I came home from work the next evening, he had set the table in the dining room for us, instead of our usual habit of eating at the small kitchen table. He had found one of my wedding presents in the sideboard, a white damask tablecloth with matching napkins, that I had only used once before. It was a present from Aunt Joan and Uncle Will and I had brought it out years ago when they came for a Sunday lunch, not long after Ricky and I married. I remembered that Ricky had been hungover from a late night DJing at a gig in London, but he still managed to make his uncle and aunt laugh at one of his outrageous stories.

I could not help comparing Guy's general domesticity and attention to detail with Ricky's total lack of interest in any household aesthetics. At one end of the dining table, Guy had placed a vase of red roses (where did he find that vase, I misplaced it years ago?) next to a bottle of Bollinger Champagne nestling in the ice bucket (another unused wedding present that had languished in the hard-to-reach high kitchen cupboard, keeping company with the fondue set and the three-tiered cake stand). He had set two places at right angles to each other, using my best silver cutlery. The matching damask napkins were folded into neat triangles and pushed into sparkling crystal wine glasses. Tall white candles in elegant silver candlesticks were placed at either end of the table and the central overhead light was dimmed. It looked inviting and a bit too intimate.

'What's all this in aid of, Guy?' I said, a little more sharply than I intended. 'Did you go out and buy those candlesticks? I don't remember seeing them before.' What was he playing at, I wondered? He was leaving soon and had obviously gone to a lot of effort, as if he were making a final push to impress me. Hopefully seduction was not on his mind. There was another part of his personality that I had become aware of and had a problem with. He was very intense about everything, childlike in his need for constant affirmation. Looking for my approval of everything he did. 'It looks lovely, Guy, but I thought you Australians specialised in barbeques and bush tucker, you know, kangaroo steaks and snags!' I added, to tease him a little and get him to relax.

He looked a bit deflated, his thinnish top lip narrowing further into a downward curve. 'You have been working so hard, Marie, I just wanted to show you my appreciation for helping me so much since Dad…' he said quietly, not laughing at my teasing comment.

I felt a bit guilty, he had gone to so much effort for me. I could smell a delicious aroma of cooking wafting in from the kitchen. It must have taken him most of the day while I was at work, to put this meal presentation together. I squeezed his arm. 'Thanks, Guy,' I said. 'You are spoiling me.'

'You deserve it, Marie.' Guy hurried into the kitchen and emerged with a casserole of coq-au-vin.

He was an enigma for sure. I had learned of his world-wide travels, often going native and living with indigenous tribes for months at a time. Or learning to scuba dive in the Philippines and becoming an instructor for the tourists. Being single, he could leave Australia on a whim and travel to the more remote areas on the planet, yet here he was, behaving like a domestic god, taking care of my every need, as if he were a house-husband. It had been a bit stultifying at times, but the champagne, and the coffee liqueur mellowed my mood and I left his arm draped over my shoulder when we finally moved into the lounge, sharing the two-seater sofa. It did not feel claustrophobic at all.

Then he was kissing me and I kissed him back. Why not? He would be leaving soon and it had been a while since I last went to bed with a man. That would have been Mark, I was thinking, but it was Ricky I was remembering as Guy took off my clothes with shaking hands. How did we get upstairs, I barely remembered? He was as intense in bed as he was about everything else. Desperate to please.

'Do you want me to do this? Does that feel good for you? Do you want to come on top of me?'

'Shh, not another word. I need to focus.' To forget who I was with. Guy's muscular body, covered in downy, reddish hair and his staccato breathing and groans were putting me off. That combined with an earlier memory of watching him inject insulin into his thigh when I had walked past his open bedroom door. I knew he was diabetic, he was diagnosed when he was a teenager, but it was disconcerting to see him casually pressing a needle into his flesh. I am so squeamish about needles. But I closed my eyes and imagined I was with Ricky again. He had been an amazing lover, funny, quirky and totally sexy, every time - at least until the drugs gradually killed off his libido. But oh, he would be enraged, if even now, after all the years of separation, he knew I had slept with his much-loathed cousin.

The last week was quickly coming to an end. The first night after we had slept together, I went upstairs early to have a long soak in the bath. I was in the middle of an exciting Margaret Attwood novel and was looking forward to catching up with the plot, followed by a deep undisturbed sleep. I was so tired. When I walked into my bedroom, Guy was sitting on the edge of my bed in his boxers, his clothes discarded on the floor at his feet.

I stopped short, feeling surprise, some shock and a flash of irritation. What the hell was he doing here? I had not invited him again to share my bed tonight. Sex with him had not been that great. All over very quickly.

'Come to bed, Marie. I'll make it up to you for last night. I was a bit too nervous...' he patted the bed and smiled.

I bit back the dismissive words I wanted to say, probably because he was being extra kind and solicitous to me, doing all the odd jobs around the house and in the garden that I had been too busy and too tired to deal with. Although it did feel as if he was trying to micro-manage my life, routines and decisions. I sighed quietly and walked to the bed. It was only for another few days. He would be gone soon.

I was feeling exhausted and had been experiencing a few tension headaches at work, so when Guy suggested that we shared a short break away before he flew back to Australia, I was surprised but agreed. I so needed a holiday. There had been a blizzard of extra work to cover at the bank as my colleague was off with a long-term illness. I assumed Guy would be planning a short package holiday in Spain. A few days in the sunshine would be just perfect, I thought.

'I've booked a safari for us in Kenya, with a couple of days at the beginning to relax in a hotel in Lamu Island just off the coast of Kenya. I've been there. Wait till you see the colour of the water, Marie! It's cobalt blue and the sand dunes are pure white, nothing like it anywhere!' Guy was quite animated.

'Heavens, Guy, I thought you would be booking a cheap package holiday in Spain for us. A Kenyan safari must have cost you a packet. That is very generous of you.'

'Marie, you have been so kind to me since Dad died. I could not have got through all of that without you. You have been amazing. A decent holiday is the least I can do to repay you.' Guy's eyes misted up.

'Well, if you insist,' I said quickly, hoping he would not break down again. 'I had better go upstairs and pack for a safari holiday then.'

Our flight left at midday. By the time we took our seats on the plane, Guy had downed a couple of beers at the bar in the departure lounge. I was surprised, for, apart from that night a week ago, when we drank the champagne and liqueurs, neither of us had touched any alcohol. It gave me a headache the next day, even when I drank lots of water, and Guy was diabetic, not too sensible of him to be drinking either. It continued on-board, he had booked us onto business class and the flight attendants were handing out drinks before the flight took off and again as soon as they reached cruising altitude and the seat belt signs were switched off. Guy was drinking white wine and whisky, helping himself off the tray every time the flight attendant walked past him.

'Guy, take it easy.' I whispered urgently, as he was

now snapping his fingers rudely for more drink to be brought to him. I could see the burly male in-flight supervisor watching us. If he gets too obstreperous, the IFS will be having strong words with him. I can't believe this. He is like a Jekyll and Hyde character when he is drunk. I've never seen this side of him before. Some holiday this will be if he behaves like a misplaced colonial every time he has a drink.

'C'mon Marie, don't be a fuddy duddy. Just chill out, we're on holiday.' His speech was slurred but he was still obnoxiously loud.

'Go to sleep, Guy and just shut up.'

'How do you expect me to sleep on these seats, they are too uncomfortable? Hey, you. I need another drink,' he shouted loudly at the flight attendant further up the aisle.

'Sir, I trust you are enjoying your flight with us today, but just to let you know that some of our passengers wish to sleep after the meal, so as a courtesy to them, perhaps you could desist from shouting at my colleague as you will disturb the other passengers. Should you require any further service for the remainder of the flight until we serve breakfast, you can deal directly with me.' The IFS was right in Guy's face as he delivered his smooth warning.

'No worries, mate,' said Guy surprisingly meekly, 'I am going to sleep now too.' He drained his glass of wine and thrust it into the IFS's hand and slouched down in his seat, eyes closed, feigning sleep.

I turned my back on him, embarrassed and appalled at his boorish behaviour. What had I done? Now that I had time to think and reflect on some of his odd ways while he was staying with me, I did begin to wonder if there was something not quite right about him. On reflection, he had swung from being very clingy at first with all his emotional outbursts and desire to please me, to subtly trying to control my life. The phone bill incident, wanting to know exactly what time I would be home, insisting on coming with me when I visited my friends, and just last night sharing my bed, his scary theatre of foreplay with his knife... now he had morphed into a loutish, ill-mannered moron, drunk and boorish. I had ignored or made excuses in my mind for his behaviour in my house, putting it down to grief and loneliness, but this drunkenness was a deal-breaker. There was no way I was prepared to spend the next ten days with him. I had to get away from him, putting up with this was not an option for me. I did not speak to him again during the rest of the flight. When we got off the plane at Kenya International

Airport, there was a two-hour stopover before our connecting flight to Lamu Airport. Guy was groggy and in a foul temper.

'Jees, I've gotta get some sleep. Wake me up when it's time to board.' He stretched himself out on the floor, pillowed his head on his rucksack and fell asleep, mouth open, rasping snores drawing disapproving looks from the other handful of passengers killing time like us for the connecting flight.

I couldn't bear looking at him and wandered off to freshen up a bit in the ladies' loo, and afterwards drank a ridiculously expensive cup of coffee, sitting precariously on a squeaky high bar stool, gazing out over the runway boundary to the orange-tinged African landscape beyond. I felt so disappointed. This should be an amazing adventure, but instead, here I was, stuck with an utter boor that I would need to find a way to dump and get back home as soon as I could. I did not have an exit plan at this point, but I would find a way. I was determined.

The announcement for our flight departure came and as our luggage was being transferred to this connecting flight, I had no choice but to continue. It would give me more time to work out what to say to him and to book myself a return flight home. Guy was now awake and propped up at the bar in the departure lounge, with a full glass of beer in his hand.

'Hurry up, Guy, our flight is boarding now. We need to go.'

'They'll have to wait till I finish my drink. I'm not rushing anywhere just to suit them.'

'Don't be ridiculous, Guy, you can't keep an aircraft waiting for you.'

'Watch me,' he said, completely refusing to budge.

'Oh, suit yourself." I left him leaning on the bar and boarded the small plane that would take us to the ferry port where we were due to catch a boat to Lamu Island.

The aircraft was ready to take off and Guy had still not appeared. I could hear the flight attendants, there were only two on this small turbo-prop aircraft, muttering about the missing passenger holding us up. So embarrassing. He eventually appeared in the doorway and blundered his way down the narrow aisle between the two rows of two seats towards me. Carelessly, he knocked into some passengers' shoulders with his swinging rucksack, totally oblivious. No apology to the flight attendants or the other passengers for keeping the plane waiting. He thumped down beside me on the aisle seat, and instinctively I shrunk away from any contact with him. By now I was finding him unbearable.

He was still hungover and bad tempered as we waited at the carousel at Lamu Airport for our luggage to appear. We were the only two people left standing by the carousel as we watched a couple of forlorn and unclaimed suitcases go round and round. The same suitcases that always seem to travel unaccompanied around the globe. Our suitcases did not appear. Guy went ballistic, shouting and gesticulating at the airline representatives. I was totally mortified by his behaviour and went off to find the loo. By the time I reappeared, he was moodily kicking his foot against the desk while the airline representative spoke rapidly into her cell phone.

'Sir and madam, please accept our sincere apologies. I assure you that your luggage will be delivered to your hotel on Lamu Island by courier tomorrow. I have arranged a limousine to drive you to the harbour. So sorry for the inconvenience.'

'It's more than an inconvenience,' Guy grumbled loudly. 'It's bloody disgraceful.'

I tugged him away. 'Thank you for helping us. We know it's not your fault.'

Fortunately, I had packed a few toiletries in my

carry-on bag and I was casually dressed for the flight in lightweight trousers and a loose blouse, as was Guy, in his usual jeans and polo shirt. We would have to make do with what we had until the next day when our missing luggage was due to arrive. The limousine dropped us off at the Mekowe Jetty and we stepped on board the African dhow that would ferry us over the short stretch of water to the Peponi Hotel. We were the only two people on the boat and Guy stuck to my side the whole way, repeatedly asking me what was wrong and why was I being so moody. I was so tired and upset with him by now that I could only answer in monosyllables, dreading having to tell him that I was pulling out of this holiday and why.

As we sailed closer to the shores of Shela, a town on the east side of Lamu Island, I could see the Peponi Hotel where Guy had booked us in. It was almost sitting on top of the pristine beach, flanked by undulating white sand dunes that shimmered with reflected late-afternoon sunlight. The hotel was a small two storey building and had been run by the same family for 50 years, as I found out by reading the brochure at the reception desk, while Guy, still stroppy and hungover, booked us in to one of their 28 double rooms. This should have been perfect, I thought regretfully. The hotel was intimate and the staff friendly, everywhere had views over the Indian Ocean and the untouched white sands, Guy was right about that. He seemed a bit calmer now that we had been shown to our luxury bedroom suite with its cool white décor, beamed ceilings and a stunning sea view from our private balcony. I was so tired from the long journey and needed a night's sleep before I faced Guy with my departure plan, and was glad to chill out on our balcony and watch the huge orange sun disappear below the horizon, exchanging the orange, pink and purple-tinted sky for a deep velvety blue, peppered with tiny flashes of light from distant constellations. It should have been magical.

Guy ordered room service for us and a bottle of red and white wine to go with the stunning selection of food, a beautifully presented seafood platter, a delightful fusion of freshly caught shellfish and colourful salad vegetables. I had a glass of the chilled white wine and then went on to fill my glass from the carafe of iced water. Guy finished the bottle of white wine and then started on the red.

'Guy, don't you think you have had enough to drink after the flight and now?' I was tentative, expecting another volatile explosion. 'Especially with your diabetes. Excess alcohol can drop your blood sugar levels dangerously low, as I am sure you know already.'

I briefly placed my hand over his large one, grasping his fingers in a conciliatory gesture to emphasise my point. He pulled his hand away and stood up.

'Stone the flamin' crows, Marie! Can't a bloke enjoy a few jars on holiday?' His face flushed and his lips thinned. 'I'm going down to the bar, see you later if you want to come down.'

Well, I tried, but that reaction just confirmed my decision that as soon as my luggage arrived, I was leaving. I was too tired to care. I had a quick shower, rinsed out my smalls and fell into the cavernous double bed, being sure to pull the mosquito nets around first. I was vaguely aware of Guy coming into the room in the small hours and collapsing in a heap on the far side of the bed, snoring out his alcohol-soured breath.

He was very quiet the next morning as we sat on our balcony sharing a huge continental breakfast. We had three different jugs of ice-cold juice, guava, pineapple and orange and a basket of still warm croissants hiding under a pristine white napkin, the usual spreads, butter and jams and a massive jug of freshly brewed coffee. Guy ruined the moment by requesting champagne to complement the orange juice. I shuddered, was he building up to another Bucks

Fizz-fuelled tirade against the world? A gentle sea breeze whispered through the flowers of the hibiscus shrubs in their large, white ceramic pots. The quietened hush of the wavelets breaking respectfully against the white sandy shore added to the sheer beauty and serenity of this paradise. It should be bliss, I mourned inside, but I had been psyching myself up since before dawn to make this speech to Guy and was even more determined now that he had started another day with alcohol. I was desperately hoping that our luggage would arrive soon. It was horrible and uncomfortable to put on my travel clothes again, but I wanted to avoid a scene in the hotel and suggested that we go for a walk along the beach. Guy stuck closely to my side as we walked towards the beach and tried to take my hand which I avoided by bending down to take off my sandals. The glistening white grains of sand filtered through my toes as I looked longingly at the clear blue water, desperate to walk straight in and cool my fevered body and mind - dreading the difficult speech I was about to make. Had to make.

'Look, Guy, I really think we would be better off finishing this holiday. I can't be with someone whose behaviour changes so dramatically with alcohol. You turn into someone I can't cope with. So aggressive, so rude to everyone! You never displayed any of this behaviour when you were staying at my house. Plus,' I continued rapidly, 'you are diabetic and excessive alcohol is dangerous for your health, you must know that yourself.'

'Aw come on, Marie, you can't be serious. I just had a few drinks. What's the problem?'

'You're the problem, Guy. I am leaving as soon as the luggage arrives.' My pulse was racing. 'This was a mistake. I never should have come on a holiday with you.'

'You're just stressed, Marie. You have been working too hard and having to look after your mum all the time. You just need to relax and get into the holiday mood. You can't just leave me.' He grasped my arm to stop me walking ahead of him, now I had said my piece. I shook off his arm and turned back towards the hotel.

He thought I was bluffing. 'What's all this fuss about, Marie? Why can't we just spend some time together? You'll feel better once you relax.'

When I did not answer and walked on, he tried another tactic, stepping in front of me, blocking my way.

'Look, Marie, I'm sorry, I think my drinking on the flight was just a build-up of all the stress over Dad and having to sell his house…' There was a catch in his voice and his pale, red-rimmed eyes, the whites cracked with a spidery network of broken capillaries, filled up with tears. 'Look, I promise not to drink any more today. Let's just have a day out exploring Lamu Old Town, you'll like that.' He held both of my hands in his, squeezing hard and gazed dolefully at me, his tears threatening to break loose from his glistening eyes.

'No, I am going back to the hotel to see if our luggage has turned up and then I am going out again to try and buy some summer clothes. I'm sweltering in these trousers. Why don't you find something else to do?' I just wanted to get away from him and his transparent attempt at trying to elicit my sympathy.

'I'm coming with you, I can't let you wander about on your own here, it's not safe. I will look after you.' His tone changed into a slurred whine.

I felt trapped and threatened by his intensity, just wanted to end it. But our luggage still had not arrived. I could not leave yet. There were no tourists on the streets, which were just dirt tracks with stalls set up in tight alleyways. No cars were allowed on the island so there was no need for proper roads. All I could find to buy were a couple of brightly coloured beach wraps, better than nothing. On the way back to the hotel, we passed a tiny restaurant. Immediately the owner accosted us. He insisted on showing us his 'rooftop restaurant' with one table. Pleading with us to come and eat there that evening. Promising us the 'best food in town'. I agreed, thinking that at least I would not have to endure the embarrassment of Guy behaving like a drunken fool again in the hotel restaurant. We got back to the hotel with a few hours to kill before the evening meal at the tiny rooftop restaurant. Guy wandered off, presumably to find the bar.

It was bliss to get out of my hot, sticky travel clothes and change into one of the beach wraps. There were hammocks slung between palm trees near the pool and I spent the rest of the afternoon gently swaying in one, reading my book and avoiding contact with Guy, who had not reappeared. I had almost dozed off when the hotel porter came to tell me that our luggage had arrived on the late afternoon boat from the mainland. At last! I would be free to leave now. Tomorrow was the start of the Safari and we would be leaving the island. Once we were back on the mainland, I would leave Guy and find a way to get back home. He had our tickets, so I would have to buy a ticket home on my credit card if he refused to give me the one he had for me. I just needed to get through this evening meal *à deux* as calmly as possible and hope that Guy would behave reasonably and not drink too much.

He was a strange fellow, completely different now that he was away from his domesticated behaviour at my house. I was glad to have been able to help him get through his recent loss and felt slightly guilty about my decision to dump him but convinced myself that his alcohol abuse made him delusional. I wished I hadn't slept with him now, but I had not given him any indication that we were in a relationship. It was just a fling and the thought of being intimate with him again repelled me. I was dreading the possibility of him attempting to get romantic with me later. Why oh why had I let myself get into this situation?

My luggage contained one dress, a softly draped hyacinth blue sleeveless shift that I had treated myself to during a last-minute dash round the stores at home. It would be good to wear it at least once. Ricky had always liked me in blue.

My face and legs were itching, little red raised bumps from sand-fly bites everywhere. I hoped a long cool shower would help. Guy's bag was open and his travel clothes scattered on the floor. He must have come back to our room earlier and showered and changed. There was no sign of him. He would be having sundowners at the bar, revving up for another night of heavy drinking and endlessly urging me to 'relax and enjoy myself'. I was dreading tonight but consoled myself that it would soon be over and that Guy could get back to Australia to his life as a loner, and where the vagaries of his strange personality were probably better understood and tolerated by the men who worked for him.

The shower felt divine on my heated skin and I just stood for a while luxuriating in the feel of the tepid water running over my head, cooling me down. I reached up for the shower gel. The pain hit my head, neck and back like a bullet, doubling me over in agony and shock. Oh my god, what the hell is this? I managed to stumble out of the shower grabbing a towel on the way. I staggered over to the bed clutching my head, this pain was unbearable. Painkillers, painkillers where are they? I fumbled for my bag on the bedside locker and groped around. I always carried a few paracetamols with me. Just in case. I had been getting a few headaches recently, but this was something else. Migraine? I had never had one before. Managed to swallow two tablets. Must lie down, maybe it will go away.

2

The Aftermath

Guy came back into the room. 'Marie, what's wrong? It's nearly time for our meal.'

Marie could smell the alcohol on his breath as he leaned over her. It made her feel sick.

'You go. Can't let the restaurant owner down. I have a bad headache. I just need… rest.'

'Are you sure? I'm hungry. I was looking forward to eating on that rooftop restaurant. Great views over the ocean.'

Stop talking, my head is killing me. 'Just go,' she managed, before another crippling spasm gripped her head in a vice.

He came back two hours later. The restaurant owner was right, the food had been great and the owner had kept him company, sharing the wine and brandy as they swapped stories about their overseas travels. Marie was still lying on the bed covered only in a towel, she was shifting about a bit and moaning. He leant over her and shook her shoulder.

'Marie, wake up. Are you all right?'

She moaned again but did not open her eyes. Her skin was flushed, she was burning up. Her head turned, hanging over the bed. Suddenly she vomited. He jumped away from her, horrified and phoned for the housekeeper to come to the room.

'Madam very sick, best we call the doctor.' The housekeeper watched concerned, as Guy paced up and down the length of the room, unable to take charge of this crisis. He left to call the doctor at the housekeeper's repeated urging. She stayed with Marie until the village doctor arrived, dealing with the frequent vomiting attacks. The doctor took her temperature and left stronger painkillers for her to take, advising Guy to take her off the anti-malaria tablets as they might be responsible for the vomiting.

'Can you get someone to stay with her please? I can't cope with this. I've just lost my father.' Guy clutched his head in his hands and slumped into one of the rattan chairs on the balcony.

The housekeeper nodded and quickly made a call on the internal phone. 'I will stay with madam, watch her for you.' She sat down on a bedside chair and throughout the night tried to understand the few words that Marie managed to mumble, but none of it made any sense. Occasionally Marie would attempt to sit up, but she had lost the ability to coordinate any movement.

'We must call the doctor again, sir. Madam still not well.'

Guy came over to the bed, he had spent the night on the balcony, drinking. 'Marie, can you hear me?'

She opened her eyes and looked at him, then she turned her head away, flapping uselessly with her hand. She managed to swallow the anti-inflammatory pills the doctor prescribed for her, as the housekeeper supported her head. The housekeeper, showing signs of fatigue after her long vigil, gently rubbed cream into the sand-fly bites on Marie's face and limbs.

'Sir, I am leaving now, but I send another girl to watch over madam. But you must stay with her too. She is very sick.'

As the morning passed, interminably slowly for

Guy, it was clear that Marie was not improving and he began to show signs of panic. He started biting his nails and paced nervously up and down the room, thoughts darting about in his mind like demented trapped flies. She was drifting in and out of awareness but was unable to move off the bed. He went through her bag and pulled out all her travel documents, passport, and insurance cover details. He contacted her insurance company to explain how ill she was and that they were on Lamu Island which did not have a suitable hospital.

'I'm her partner,' he told them. 'Can you arrange accommodation for me near the hospital in Nairobi?' he asked, after arrangements were made to get them off the island to Nairobi Hospital.

There was no boat due for a few hours so the only way to get Marie back to the mainland was on a small African dhow. She was only partly aware of how precarious that part of the journey was. She had to be carried onto the boat up a rickety plank, supported by two wiry local islanders and deposited none too gently on a pallet for the mercifully short sail over to the mainland. Then she was loaded onto an air-ambulance, another bumpy ride in a two-propeller small plane, to an airfield near the hospital. The final leg of her journey was in a properly equipped ambulance, driving at night, to finally deliver her to Nairobi Hospital, six hours after she left Lamu Island.

She remained semi-conscious and fully aware of the excruciating pain in her head and the pressure behind her eyes. Try as she might, she could not find the words to express her fear. What was happening to her? She was vaguely conscious of Guy in her peripheral vision, sitting with his head buried in his hands. Was he sobbing? She closed her eyes against the pain and disquiet. All became quiet and dark, her awareness suspended.

She remembered very little of the next two days. She heard words: blood tests, angiogram, brain scan. Was vaguely aware of her bed being moved around, heard voices explaining what was happening but made no sense of it, felt hands repositioning her body, waves of pain squeezing inside her head and behind her eyes, sharp sting in her arm. Where was she? Where is my daughter? I want to hear Sally's voice. She can tell me what's happening to me.

She hears the word aneurysm. Urgent voices. Feels fear. My dad died of an aneurysm. Am I dying? Sally, Sally, where are you?

It took five days of tests before Marie was finally diagnosed with a subarachnoid haemorrhage. The weakened blood vessel in her brain had burst, she needed urgent surgery to clip the vessel and stop the bleeding. Her condition was deteriorating but she would have to be transferred to Johannesburg 3000 kilometres away, where the skills of an experienced neuro-surgeon would be required to perform the delicate operation. She existed in a sea of pain, pressure and confusion and had no understanding of what was happening to her. Guy drifted in and out of her awareness. She closed her eyes, turning away from his intense, staring gaze. No comfort for her, just fear.

It was midday before the ambulance appeared to transport Marie, barely conscious, to Nairobi airport, then the flight to a small airport near the hospital in Johannesburg and another 45-minute ambulance ride to the private Sunningdale Hospital where she was immediately admitted to the Intensive Care Unit, her burst aneurysm still leaking deadly amounts of blood into her brain. Guy was distraught, just sobbing and incoherent, unable to provide any useful information about Marie's medical history to the team of medics urgently trying to assess her. He left with their bags to find the address of the hotel near the hospital that the insurance company had found for him.

3

Fiona, Johannesburg

'Madam Fiona, can you try to speak with this lady please? We think she is English, but she is not making any sense and very agitated and we can't get her to take her medication. Her brain is in spasm with infection, we need to get it under control before we can operate. She is dangerously ill. Her husband, he no use, just crying like a baby. He says her name is Marie.' The nurse pointed out the small, slight figure of the woman lying in the corner bed of the ICU ward.

Fiona was well-known by the hospital staff. She and her husband, Graham, ran a private guesthouse, Westford, a forty-minute drive away from the hospital. A few years earlier she had signed contracts with several of the big construction and mining companies in neighbouring Angola to look after any of their ex-patriot workers requiring private medical treatment at Sunninghill Hospital. Fiona or Graham would pick them up from the airport, take them to their guesthouse and transport them back and forth to the hospital for operations and follow-up visits as required. Almost daily, Fiona would be at the hospital either visiting one of her "wounded soldiers" as she called them or taking patients back to her guesthouse to recuperate. The hospital staff completely trusted her. She was on her way home when the worried nurse had stopped her. She looked over at the forlorn figure in the corner bed and her big generous heart filled with compassion.

She often reflected on how she had morphed from a dynamic businesswoman running a highly successful designer lingerie company, into the owner of what was once a large family home now converted into a sought-after guesthouse. The house had also been the nerve centre of her prodigious creativity of new designs for her silk lingerie and where she held business meetings with her out-of-town buyers.

Fiona also loved cooking, and often she would entertain her business contacts with an evening meal and frequently, they would be invited to sleep over, rather than her or her husband driving them back late at night to their hotels. A much safer solution in those troubled post-apartheid days in Johannesburg. They had extended the house for Fiona's parents to come and live with them after Fiona's mother's export business was raided and she had a gun held to her head and all her employees had been tied up. Not surprisingly, the poor woman lost her confidence and after living quietly with Fiona and her husband, Graham, for a few years, her parents decided to retire back to Scotland. Fiona too had a few scary experiences while driving around to outlying business premises through politically unstable and volatile townships where violence could erupt in a heartbeat. That forced her to change direction and slow down the frenetic and potentially dangerous pace she lived her life at and the risks she was now exposed to.

She was considering giving up when one of her business contacts asked her if she would look after his wife who was having an operation while he was on an overseas trip. He told Fiona that his wife was very nervous about the surgery and would need to convalesce for a few days. It would mean a lot to him if she could help him out.

'Don't you worry, I will look after her for you,' she

had promised. She collected the woman from the airport, and took her straight to the hospital for her pre-op assessment. She stayed with her until she was settled into her private room, went back the next morning and sat with her, reassuring her and keeping her calm until she was wheeled off, heavily sedated for the surgery, and was there when the woman came back from recovery and woke up. It was years since Fiona had felt so at peace with herself. This, she realized that day, was what she wanted to do with her life.

'Graham, pet, let's turn this house into a proper guesthouse,' she said to her devoted husband. 'I have been told that there are plenty of expats coming to Sunninghill Hospital from Angola and they are always looking for somewhere safe to recuperate.'

Graham was delighted. He worried about his wife and the risks she took driving around. He knew Fiona could not bear to be idle. Running a guesthouse would keep her busy and safe. The conversions took a while, Graham was in his element, he loved big projects. During that time, Fiona signed three contracts with international companies to look after their executives on business trips or to care for employees having operations. In the end, some guests would stay for up to three months, many coming back for further visits. Fiona and Graham hosted guests from several different nationalities and their home became a haven for expats, thousands of miles away from their own countries and cultures. It seemed to Fiona that people were really all the same under the skin, all needing warmth, companionship and laughter in their lives, regardless of any cultural differences.

Fiona sat down at the woman's bedside and took the small cold hand in hers, making sure not to disturb the positioning of the hydra-headed cannula protruding obscenely from the translucent skin on the back of Marie's hand.

'Hi, Marie, I'm Fiona. Can you hear me?' There was no response, just rapid eye movement behind the closed lids, bluish, bruised veils against the pale, English rose complexion. She sat quietly, holding Marie's hand. She would have to be patient, but time was not on her side. This woman was dying. She looked up and saw the tall bulk of a man approaching the bed. His hair was ruffled in a wild sandy-coloured tangle, his pale eyes puffy with dark circles underneath. He stopped at the other side of the bed and glared suspiciously at Fiona as she continued to hold Marie's hand.

'Who are you?' he asked as he grabbed Marie's other hand possessively.

Fiona explained in a quiet voice who she was and that the nurses had asked her to try and find out more about Marie, and to try and persuade her to take the medication which would clear the infection and spasms before they dared operate.

'I presume you are her husband?' She gave him one of her direct looks, designed to connect.

He nodded, his eyes filling up with tears. 'Yes, I'm Guy,' he managed.

'The nurses said you were too upset to give them any information about her. Maybe you could talk to me? She desperately needs surgery, but her brain is in spasm. Do you know if she is allergic to anything?'

Guy immediately put his hands over his eyes and his whole body shook with emotion. 'I can't think straight, I'm so worried about my wife, but the insurance company has put me into this crook hotel. It's a hell hole of a place. Noisy, dirty, awful.' Guy started sobbing.

'Look, go and collect your bags, check out and come back here. You can come and stay at my guesthouse until your wife has her operation.'

Guy immediately pulled himself together and shook Fiona's hand. 'Fair dinkum, Fiona? That's really kind of you. I don't know what I will do if anything happens to her. I just lost my dad recently.' His lips trembled dangerously again. 'See you later.' He ambled off and Fiona resumed her vigil at Marie's bedside until he returned an hour or two later with their two rucksacks. She thought she could smell alcohol on his breath. She took him back to her guesthouse and cooked him a hot meal. He told her he had not had a hot meal for days and that he had run out of money.

The next day Fiona drove Guy to the hospital. Marie's eyes were open, but she still did not speak.

'Hello, darling, how are you?' When she heard his voice and saw Guy's face inches from hers as he leant over to kiss her cheek, she turned her head away from him and stared wide-eyed at Fiona and weakly tried to squeeze Fiona's hand.

'What's wrong with her?' He looked at Fiona, distressed. 'I can't cope with this. I'll come again tomorrow. Maybe she will be more settled then. I'll wait for you in the cafeteria.' He hesitated a moment, then said, 'Don't suppose you could lend me a few rand, just until I can get some funds transferred from Australia?'

'Of course, Guy, no problem.' Fiona quickly gave him the rand notes in her purse. He shoved the money into his back pocket and left.

Fiona was puzzled, Marie seemed agitated, but she let Fiona hold her hand and managed to squeeze Fiona's hand feebly. Her lips moved but no sound came out. Then, as if the effort was just too much, her eyes drooped shut and she fell asleep. Fiona left soon after, hopeful that tomorrow, Marie might manage to speak to her. Something didn't feel right. Why did the sight of Guy upset Marie? Unless of course it was the effects of the haemorrhage affecting her memory? Impossible to guess.

Fiona was desperate to get back to the hospital as early as possible the next day. The duty nurse had called her in the middle of the night to tell her that Marie was awake but refusing to take the medication. It was critical, the nurse said, as they needed to get the brain spasms and the infection under control before they could operate. Graham, her husband, said he would bring Guy over to the hospital later that morning, placidly accepting his wife's pre-dawn rush back to Marie's bedside.

'Hello again. It's Fiona, remember?'

Marie's eyes were wide open today. 'Where is my daughter? I want to see Sally. Tell her I'm here please.' The words come out in a desperate whisper through her dry lips.

Fiona squeezed her hand, leaning closer to Marie's face, smiling. 'It's going to be all right,' she said gently, reassuringly. 'Your husband, Guy, is coming to see you in a wee while.'

'No! No! He's not my husband. Keep him away from me!' Agitated, Marie clutched at Fiona's hand, but before Fiona could say anything else, Marie slipped back into her unconscious world.

Fiona was uneasy, Guy had not mentioned that Marie had a daughter, and what did she mean saying that Guy wasn't her husband? Was Marie just delusional from her fevered brain? But something about this did not feel right. She couldn't allow Guy near Marie until she found out more about this relationship and if there was indeed a daughter called Sally.

Fiona phoned Graham and told him not to bring Guy to the hospital until she got back. 'I'll explain when I see you,' she told him. 'I just need to wait and try to get Marie to take her medication when she wakes up again.'

When Marie woke up, Fiona focused on persuading her to swallow the medication. 'Marie, your daughter, Sally, would want you to take the medicine to help you get better. Will you take it now from the nurse?' Marie nodded her head, grimacing as the movement shot another shard of pain across her forehead. Fiona beckoned the nurse to come over, and between them they gently eased Marie's head off the pillow so she could swallow more easily. Fiona was appalled at how fragile and almost transparent Marie seemed. Blue veins at her temples were pulsing under the pressure from the blood seeping out of the leaking aneurism and her eyes seemed glazed, although she managed to focus on Fiona who smiled and nodded encouragingly.

'Well done, Marie, if you keep taking the medication you will soon feel much better and I promise I will get Sally here as soon as possible.'

Marie managed a faint smile then her eyes closed again, even before they placed her head gently back on the pillow.

Fiona drove at breakneck speed back to the guesthouse, flooded with a mixture of fear for Marie's life, ebbing away with each day that passed, and rage and frustration with Guy's obfuscation. Clearly, he was withholding vital information about Marie's family. What the hell was the matter with him? She was determined to confront him. As soon as she drove through the security gates at the entrance to the long driveway, still driving too fast and skidding to a halt at the steps leading up to the front door, she ran breathlessly up the steps and straight up to Guy's room on the first landing. She knocked and pushed his door open without waiting. Guy was sitting hunched on his bed, his large hands clutched between his knees, head down staring at the floor.

'What's going on, Guy? Marie spoke today. She said you are not her husband and to keep you away from her.' She stood in the doorway, her arms folded, not prepared to budge until she got some explanation from him. 'Is it true, are you not really her husband? She wants to see her daughter. Does she have a daughter, Sally? And why have you not mentioned that?' Fiona could feel all her ancestral Scottish rage against betrayals flaring out to this man who had scared that vulnerable wee soul, lying so close to death in the hospital.

Guy lifted his head but did not make eye contact with Fiona. 'OK! OK! I am not her husband – yet. But we were going to get engaged on this holiday and she was coming back to Australia to live with me. It… it just seemed easier to say we were married when she had to go to hospital, otherwise they might not have given me access to her.' He looked at Fiona now, tears welling in his puckered eyes, his face illuminated by the early morning rays of sunshine piercing through his bedroom window.

'What about her daughter? How could you not have told Sally? Marie might die!' Fiona's voice rose in frustration and anger and she glared at Guy, furious with him now.

'Sally hates me, she's jealous and wants to split us up. None of her family like me, you know, they will just try and take her away from me.' Guy was blustering now. 'Anyway, I didn't have their contact numbers to get in touch.'

'This is unbelievable, surely there must be some information in Marie's possessions. Give me her rucksack so I can have a look.' Fiona stepped further into the room and Guy suddenly reared up off the bed, pushing the two rucksacks behind him.

'No! There's nothing in her bag, I've already had a look.' He seemed huge and menacing now, filling the space with his bulk.

Fiona felt a frisson of fear, but she squared up to him. 'I want you to leave my house, Guy. If you are not Marie's husband, then you can find somewhere else to live. I won't have liars under my roof.'

'No! I'm not leaving until Marie has her surgery

and I know what's going to happen to her. I love her, we were going to be married. I can't leave.' Guy glared at Fiona, he was determined. She wanted access to Marie's rucksack, so she decided to back down for the moment.

'I shall tell the hospital staff that you are not her husband. I would advise you to stay away from there for now until I find a way to contact her family. They need to know how ill she is and give permission for her to have surgery.' She slammed his door on the way out. What a nutcase, she thought, and doubled her determination to keep him away from Marie. Quickly she told her husband what Guy had confessed. 'Sorry sweetheart, I need to go back to the hospital to try and question Marie. Can you hold the fort for me and give the guests breakfast? I should be back by lunchtime. Keep Guy here whatever you do but don't get into a confrontation with him. I think he is a wee bit unpredictable.'

*

Marie opened her eyes slowly and immediately recognized the now-familiar features of her daily visitor. Fiona held her hand.

'Marie,' she said calmly hiding the desperate urgency behind her questions, 'do you have an address book with your daughter's number with you? I can call her for you.'

'Yes... rucksack... green address... book. Please call my daughter, Sally, my brother...' Marie drifted off again, the effort of talking, too much for her swollen brain.

Fiona hurried over to speak to the doctors just starting their mid-morning rounds. 'Excuse me. I have something very important to tell you. The man who visits the English lady with the brain injury is not her husband and he must be kept away from her. I think he is not mentally stable. She has family in the UK and I am going home now to try to contact them.'

'Thank you for that, madam. She urgently needs surgery, we need someone to sign the consent form today, but now, she could die if we don't operate soon. Will you sign for her?' The consultant looked perplexed.

'I can't do that, I am not her next of kin. I must let her family know.' Agitated, Fiona drove furiously back to the guesthouse determined to get hold of Marie's rucksack - somehow.

She could hear the shower running in the en-suite bathroom. Praying Guy was taking a long shower, she listened at his bedroom door. Nothing else, except the sound of her heart hammering in her chest. Carefully, she opened his bedroom door. She would have to be quick. She searched around frantically, where the hell was it? She heard the shower being turned off. Desperately, she dropped to the floor and looked under his bed. There it was. She grabbed it and ran to the door, pulling it shut quietly behind her, just managing to reach the stairs before the bathroom door clicked open.

She found the green address book pushed deep into an inside flap of the rucksack under neatly folded underwear and socks. Quickly, with shaking hands, Fiona opened the address book, hoping to make an accurate guess at which entry might be Marie's brother or her daughter. Yes, Sally, her name was Sally. But the first name she came across was William Carreras, his original address crossed out a few times and replaced with subsequent ones. The most recent entry was an address in Islington. That might be her brother, it was obviously someone she kept in touch with.

'Hello, is that William Carreras?'

'Yes, who is this?

'Mr Carreras, my names is Fiona, I am calling you from Johannesburg. Do you have a sister called Marie?' She crossed her fingers.

'Yes, I do. What is it? Has something happened to her?' William had picked up on the urgency in Fiona's voice.

She went on to explain what had happened and that Marie was in urgent need of brain surgery and could he contact her daughter, Sally, and travel out as soon as possible to sign the consent forms. She also explained that Marie was with a chap called Guy who claimed that he and Marie were getting engaged, but he had been behaving strangely and had not told the doctors that Marie had family in the UK.

'OK, Fiona, I can contact Sally and my aunt and uncle who will be free to come out immediately. I will get over as soon as I can. Just to put you in the picture, Guy is Marie's cousin-in-law.'

*

It was a further two days before Marie's daughter, Sally, and her aunt and uncle arrived as they had to arrange flights and vaccinations. Marie's condition was deteriorating rapidly and Fiona was terrified that she would die before her family could see her. She spent hours at Marie's bedside, holding her hand as she slipped more frequently in and out of awareness, and praying that Marie would hold on to life. She just had to.

'Marie, your daughter, Sally, and your aunt and uncle are on their way to the hospital to see you. You will be fine now, but the doctor wants you to take more medicine so that he can operate on your head to make the pain go away. Will you do that?'

'Sally's coming, Aunt Mary and Uncle Jo coming? Good, going home.' Marie let Fiona support her head as she managed to swallow a sip of water to wash down the medication and exhausted with the pain and the effort, she slipped into another semi-comatose state.

Only then did Fiona dare to leave her side to rush to the airport to meet Marie's family who had been told by Marie's brother, William, that Fiona would collect them. She recognized Sally first, petite with shoulder-length dark curly hair, her big brown eyes dark-rimmed and fearful. She was flanked by an elderly couple, Aunt Mary and Uncle Jo, both looking worn-out and anxious.

Fiona greeted them warmly. 'I am so pleased you are here, I will take you straight to the hospital to see Marie and to sign the consent forms for her operation.'

4

Sally

Sally did not have a clue who Fiona was or how she was involved with her mother, but she sounded sincere and seemed to be up to date with Marie's condition. All Sally and the family knew was that Marie had suffered a brain bleed and was now seriously ill, but they had no idea where and when it had happened and Sally was desperate for answers. Fiona told them all she knew. Sally was horrified to learn that Marie had been in hospital in Nairobi for five days before being transferred to Johannesburg. Fiona also hinted at Guy's strange behaviour but warned Sally to stay calm around him and to try and find out all the details about what had happened to Marie.

'I can't understand why she would have gone on holiday with him. Dad hated Guy and Mum knew that.' Sally was clearly angry and confused. 'And why in heaven's name did he not let me know as soon as it happened?'

'I know, love, but as I said, just try to keep a cool head until you can question him about it. He won't talk to me sensibly about anything, just keeps breaking down.' Fiona didn't mention Guy's obsessive and brutal determination not to be side-lined by Marie's family. That would not be helpful at this stage. She could tell that Sally had a short fuse and that there would be no love lost between Sally and her loathed second cousin.

Marie's eyes brimmed with tears when she opened her eyes and saw Sally, Mary and Jo at her bedside. Clearly, she recognized them, but she could not speak coherently, although she seemed to be saying 'home now' and reached out for Sally's hand.

'Mum,' Sally bent over Marie, kissing her forehead, 'you are in hospital and the doctor needs to operate on your head to get you well. But we are all here now and you will be fine. We will take you home soon. OK?'

Marie smiled, holding firmly onto Sally's hand, but soon her grip loosened and she fell asleep again.

But they could not operate that day. Marie still had a high fever and her brain was in spasm. Sally, Mary and Jo had a conference with the surgeons who explained that as it was well over a week since the aneurysm had burst and that blood was still leaking into Marie's brain, she could die during the surgery - unless they could successfully stop the bleeding - or she might be irreversibly brain damaged. They warned the family that they may have to arrange to fly her body home to the UK. Aunt Mary was a retired cardiac nurse, she understood only too clearly how grave the situation was and that there was a high chance that Marie might not survive.

'No! No! You can't let that happen. My mother is strong. She will get better. Please, please, operate on her as soon as possible.' Sally pleaded desperately with the surgeons, her dark eyes flashing pain and fear.

Fiona came over and put her arm round Sally. 'Come on, let me take you and Jo and Mary back to my place, I have plenty room for all of you and you can come back later to see your mum. We can cancel your hotel booking, it is not too salubrious at that place anyway. It is a great comfort to your mum just knowing that you are here. She has been desperate to see you all. You probably worked out that Guy is staying at my place too. But your mum does not want to see him. Something must have happened between them to make her so agitated around him.'

On reflection, the family thought it bizarre to be putting their trust in this total stranger who had taken command of them so quickly and was now driving them back to her place to stay with her. But Fiona simply exuded such positive energy and she had been looking after Marie's wellbeing before they arrived. They had no choice but to have confidence in her.

On the journey to the guesthouse, Fiona told them that Guy had not wanted to part with Marie's bag and how she had acquired it to find the address book, but no other documents, just clothes. By the time they arrived, Sally was ready to do battle with Guy. Uncle Jo and Aunt Mary had not met him before, but they advised Sally just to stay calm until they found out from Guy what had happened to Marie.

They were in Fiona's big open-plan kitchen, sitting on bar stools, having a cup of tea when Guy walked in looking sheepish. Sally totally forgot the advice she had been given about staying calm around Guy and immediately stood up and challenged him.

'Why didn't you contact me straightaway to tell me that Mum was so ill?' She was shaking with anger. 'She could have had surgery days ago. If she dies it will be your fault!' Her fists clenched, she so wanted to deck him.

Guy's mouth was twitching and he shook his head vigorously. 'No, you don't understand.' His speech was hesitant but defensive. 'We were going to get engaged. I didn't know that she was so ill until we went to the hospital in Nairobi and they took a few days to diagnose a brain bleed. I was confused and upset.'

'I don't care and I can't think for a minute that Mum would get engaged to YOU. Give me Mum's passport and her insurance documents. WE will be looking after her affairs now. She does not want to see you. You stay away from her!' Sally's voice pitched higher and angry tears threatened to blur her vision.

'You don't get it, you little witch. We are in love and I am going to make sure that the insurance company pays out for her treatment. I am in touch with them. Don't think you can split us up, because you won't succeed.' As Guy's tone become louder and threatening, he took a step towards Sally.

'Right, that's enough!' Uncle Jo, also a big heavy-set man, stepped between them. 'Our priority here is for Marie's welfare. Let's just keep calm until we find out when they can operate on her. We can sort out the paperwork later.'

After that, Guy avoided Sally and the family as much as possible. He spent the evenings in the guesthouse bar, drinking and talking with whoever was available, relaying his poor-me story to the captive audience of businessmen and recovering expats convalescing at Westford after their surgeries. He talked Fiona's son, Jamie, into giving him a lift to the hospital, but the staff would not let him near Marie. They were all aware that he had lied about being her husband and that she got agitated when she saw him. He was furious and loitered in the cafeteria waiting for news of her pending operation.

It was four more days before Marie was stable enough for the neurosurgeon and his team to operate on her and again they warned the family that the procedure might not be successful, particularly as so many days had now passed since the original brain bleed. They should be prepared for her not surviving the surgery. During that time, Sally refused to leave her mother's bedside and sat beside her, holding her hand and talking softly and reassuringly to Marie whenever she woke up. But it was clear that Marie was deteriorating. She was able to make eye contact with Sally and would manage a weak smile and a squeeze of

Sally's hand when Sally spoke to her but she was unable to speak, and the effort of staying awake exhausted her. Fiona, and Marie's aunt and uncle, would relieve Sally at her mum's bedside vigil when she let them, but she only took short breaks at a time and insisted on sleeping in a bedside chair every night.

Finally, the neurosurgeons decided that Marie was stable enough to operate and the family waited anxiously in the family waiting room. After four hours, the neurosurgeon, still in his scrubs came to talk to them. Sally was consumed with nerves and emotion that her great aunt and uncle had been unable to contain, although they too were feeling the strain.

'The operation was successful, we have clipped the aneurism and stopped the bleeding. However, the next twenty-four hours are critical, she will be back in the ICU and closely monitored, but we won't know until she wakes up completely, how much damage has been done and what impairments she might have.' He turned to Sally who was staring wild-eyed at him. 'You should be aware that your mother has survived a near-fatal haemorrhage and that it could take a long time for her to recover from the damage this has caused to her brain. She is going to need a lot of care from now on. She will not be well enough to fly back to the UK for some time and will need a rehabilitation programme. We do have rehabilitation units she could stay in here.'

Sally nodded wordlessly at all this information. She was overwhelmed. How was she going to support her mother and help her to recover in a foreign country away from all that was familiar to both? Fiona had just joined them in the family room and heard what the neurosurgeon was saying. She stepped forward and put her arm lightly round Sally's shoulder.

'Marie and her daughter will be staying with me after she is discharged and until she is well enough to return home. We will bring her back for follow-up appointments and any specific rehabilitation exercises that the physiotherapists need to oversee. Everything else we will provide at my guesthouse.' Fiona spoke with incontrovertible authority and the neurosurgeon simply nodded in agreement.

'Very well if you are sure. I expect she will thrive better in more comfortable surroundings than in our rehabilitation clinics. If you have any more questions or concerns speak to Dr Yomo, my registrar, who will be taking care of her until she is ready to be discharged, or phone my secretary at my clinic in Johannesburg. Tomorrow I fly out to Singapore for a medical conference, but I can be contacted of course.'

Sally, much to the surgeon's mild consternation, flung her arms round his waist. 'Thank you, Dr Zorio, for saving my mother. I could not bear to lose her.'

Dr Zorio gently removed himself from Sally's strong embrace and backed out of the room, saying as he left, 'We have done our best for her surgically, the rest of her recovery will depend on the support you can all give her.'

'Sally, please come back with me now and get some rest. Your mother is in an induced coma for twenty-four hours to give her brain a chance to recover, so she won't be awake until this time tomorrow at least. I spoke to the doctors before I came in here. Everybody, come back now and have something decent to eat and get a good night's sleep. There is nothing more we can do for Marie now.' Obediently, the exhausted family followed Fiona towards the exit.

'Fiona, stop, I want to see Mum before I leave the hospital, just to be sure that she is alive,' Sally implored.

'Sorry, of course you do, Sally, but be prepared for a bit of a shock at her appearance.' Fiona warned.

Marie was still in the recovery room and the nurse

told Sally that she could only stay for a minute and that she was not to touch her mother.

Sally's hand flew up to cover her mouth, holding back the sob that strangled in her throat at the sight of Marie, her head swathed in thick bandages covering most of her forehead. One side of her face was already tinged with purple bruising and a grotesque-looking drainage tube poked out of the bandages on one side of her head. Sally could see the pinkish fluid dripping steadily down the tube into a collecting bag with measurements printed on the plastic. Marie's eyes were still taped closed and the back of both her hands had cannulas inserted with tubes attached to drip stands. She looked so tiny and helpless and the tears streamed down Sally's cheeks. But she noticed the slight rise and fall of Marie's chest under the tightly stretched white sheet.

'Oh, Mum, I'm so sorry. Thank God you are breathing.' Sally took one final look at her mother's still form and slowly walked out to join the others who were waiting anxiously for her at the exit. The cool night air washed over her as she gratefully followed Fiona and her great aunt and uncle to the car.

Just as they hit the motorway, one of Johannesburg's spectacular thunderstorms lit up the car's interior with a huge flash of sheet lightening followed seconds later by a massive, booming clap of thunder. Sally instinctively covered her ears and squeezed her eyes shut. Thank goodness her mum was missing this, she hated thunderstorms back home in England which were mild compared to this. Was this some celestial message for Marie? Sally could only hope.

'Don't worry this will be over before we reach home. They never last too long normally,' said Fiona, blinking rapidly as another flash of lightening lit up the road ahead, almost blinding her. She gritted her teeth and pushed on, hoping that this storm would not bring down trees to block the roads as had happened recently. They just needed to get home safely. Nobody said much on the drive back, all lost in their own thoughts about what might lie ahead for Marie in the weeks and months to come. Fiona was right, the storm faded into the distance and no rain followed.

Fiona was silently plotting how quickly she could get Guy out of her house now that Marie's operation was over. The last thing Marie needed was to have that psycho anywhere near her while she was recovering, Fiona thought grimly, as the car turned into the driveway and they all saw the looming shape of Guy watching for their return at the lit window of the front room. He had been hovering around the hospital earlier in the day but had come back to the guesthouse at some stage after Marie was taken into the operating theatre.

Guy came rushing out of the door and hurtled down the steps towards them breathing in short loud gasps. Sally took an involuntary step backwards to stand beside Uncle Jo who was still heaving himself out of the front passenger seat of Fiona's big estate car.

'How is she? Have you seen her? Is she awake? I have been demented with worry!' Guy pushed his hands into his hair, squeezing deep furrows between his eyes. He was staring intently at Sally. Uncle Jo placed a protective arm around her shoulders. Fiona quickly stepped forward and grasped Guy by his arm, trying to steer him back to the house.

'Calm down, Guy. Let's get in and we will tell you what we know.' He pulled his arm out of Fiona's firm grip, twisting round to glare at Sally.

'Did you see her, Sally?' His voice almost sounded like the hiss of a snake and his eyes narrowed, never leaving Sally's face.

'Yes, I did see her, the operation is over, no thanks to you. You can go away now. You are not needed here.' Sally glared back at him, her voice hoarse and cold. 'We will look after Mum from now on.'

Guy did not reply but stared, unblinking, at her for a few seconds before turning his back and going quickly up the stairs and disappearing into the bar area.

After Marie's relatives ate a meal with Fiona and her husband Graham, they retired to their rooms, exhausted and wrung out with the tension and anxiety of the last few days. Sally told Fiona that she was determined to get all Marie's documents back from Guy, but that she would tackle him the following day. She was just too tired to deal with anything else until she had a sleep.

'Right, Guy, we need to get you booked on a flight home as soon as possible. Do you have an open return ticket to Australia?' Fiona did not waste any time in letting Guy know that it was time for him to leave now that Marie's operation was over.

'I can't go home now. I will be going back to Marie's house. I need to be there to look after her when she comes home. She will want that. We were living together you know, before... before...' Guy trailed off, his pale eyes welling up again with tears. He was nursing a whisky and judging by his slurred speech and shaking hand, he had had quite a few already.

I don't believe this, thought Fiona, he can't be serious. 'No, Guy,' Fiona tried to sound patient, 'she won't need you to look after her. It may be weeks, months even, before she is fit enough to fly home. You need to go back to Australia. You have a business to run there, don't you?'

'Oh, there's no worries about the business. My team of blokes know what they're doing. They can get on with it without me being there.' Guy's grip tightened on his glass as he gazed at a spot on the marble tiled floor at Fiona's feet. 'I will need to go back to Marie's house first anyway, my gear is there.'

Fiona held back her irritation. 'Do you have Marie's house keys, Guy?' she asked casually.

'Yup. I've got all her stuff. I know you took her rucksack Fiona, but I have her passport, tickets and insurance documents. It's down to me to sort everything out for her.' Guy looked up at Fiona, a leering, triumphant smile now creasing up the puffy flesh on his face.

Fiona played her ace. 'Tell you what, Guy. You can talk it all over with Marie's brother, William. He is arriving from the UK tomorrow evening.' She left him sitting on his own at the bar, staring into his drink.

They were all just finishing breakfast the next

morning before going back to the hospital to see Marie. Fiona had phoned in very early to be told that Marie had a comfortable night and had been brought out of the induced coma. She was awake and responsive and that they could come in to visit her in the Intensive Care Unit. Fiona had told them about the crazy exchange she had with Guy the night before.

'What a moron! Who does he think he is?' Sally immediately flared up.

'Don't get too worked up about it Sally. I'm sure your Uncle William will sort him out when he arrives this evening.' Fiona was keen to calm her down before Guy appeared. 'Just try to ignore him, he'll be gone soon. Let's get going to the hospital.'

Sally lingered over a second cup of coffee while the others left the breakfast room. She was churning up inside about Guy holding on to her mum's documents and house keys. How dare he!

Guy walked through the door and she went for him, fired up with rage and indignation. Completely fearless. No way was she prepared to wait for her Uncle William to take him on.

'Give me Mum's passport and insurance documents, Guy. You have no right to have them. And the house keys as well.' They were alone. Her heart was beating faster than she would have liked, but she was in control.

He loomed over her, so close that she could smell the stale whisky on his breath and the whiff of male sweat from his shirt. His eyes were narrowed and puffy, the sandy lashes sticking out from the swollen lids like wet spikes. He looked around quickly, checking that they were alone. 'You little cunt. You are just jealous. Marie told me you would try and break us up. We love one another. Not like that bastard of a father of yours. I would never run out on her like he did. I have the keys because I live at her house now. You have no authority over me so just back off, bitch.' It was bordering on a tirade and he was in her face now.

'You are insane if you think anyone is going to believe you now. You are a total liar. If you don't hand over Mum's keys and documents, I will report you to the police here. You wouldn't enjoy a stay in a South African jail, would you?' Sally stepped back from him, fully prepared to karate chop his beefy arm if he came any closer.

'If your mum tells me herself to hand over the keys then I will, otherwise forget it. We are a couple and she loves me.' Guy gave Sally a crooked, simpering smile and walked out of the room, just as Fiona came back in, looking for her.

*

Marie looked grotesque as she lay slightly propped up on the bed in the ICU ward. One side of her face was completely swollen and purple with bruising. Both eyes were puffy and almost closed, but Sally could see the glint of recognition in the tiny, visible slits of her mother's eyes. The thick bandage on her head had been removed to expose a horrific slash of black staples running diagonally on her brow, along her hairline, finishing halfway across one side of her scalp. A thin cotton skull cap covered some of the poor shaved head where the dark lustrous curls once dominated.

'Oh, Mum, Mum.' Sally bent over so that Marie could see her without having to turn her head. 'Can you see me, Mum? Can you talk?' Sally was in turmoil. What if her mother did not know who she was? If she could not speak? But she kept her voice gentle and reassuring, taking Marie's hand and resting it against her cheek. 'You have had an operation on your head to take away the pain. I will look after you now, Mum, until you can come home. I promise.'

Marie pressed her fingers softly into Sally's cheek

and managed to whisper. 'Thank you Sallykins.' Then her eyes closed and she slept.

Tears ran down Sally's cheeks unchecked. Her mother knew who she was and understood what Sally had said. *Sallykins*, the silly pet name Marie sometimes called her when she was still living at home. It had always irritated Sally when Marie called her that, but right now, it was wonderful to hear. She would have to be patient and make sure Marie really understood what Guy was up to and was able to tell him to hand over the keys and documents. It could take some time.

Sally stayed at her mother's bedside all that first day after the operation. Marie would wake up for a few minutes at a time and manage to speak a few more words. Mary, Jo and Fiona all visited her briefly in the ICU ward and Marie recognized them and managed a weak smile and a few more words, although she was confused and unclear what had happened to her.

Early the following morning Sally and her Uncle William arrived at Marie's bedside. William had flown in very late the previous evening and had not yet seen Guy, who was keeping a low profile. However, he had been told about Guy's refusal to hand over the keys, but agreed that it would be easier if Marie could speak to him herself. Despite Fiona's misgivings and Sally's total disgust, none of Marie's family knew for sure what the real relationship between Guy and Marie was. Marie seemed more alert and smiled happily at William, her oldest brother.

'Sally, Will, so pleased…' Marie's voice trailed off, but she held her brother's hand tightly as Sally bent over to gently kiss the livid bruising on her mother's face.

Carefully, Sally explained that Guy had the keys to Marie's house and that he said he was living there with her. Marie reacted immediately.

'No, not true… Australia… lives Australia.' Her fingers dug into Sally's hand.

'It's all right, Mum. If I can get him to the phone do you think you could manage to tell him to hand over the keys?'

'Yes,' said Marie, her voice the strongest it had been so far. Then she fell asleep.

Sally arranged to call the guesthouse when Marie woke up again and Fiona would bring Guy to the phone to speak to Marie. It was a gamble, as Sally was not sure if Marie would be articulate enough to convince Guy to hand everything over and leave. But somehow, Marie managed to say quite clearly to Guy that he must give the documents and house keys to Fiona.

'Go home, Guy, my family… here… take care of me.' Sally held the phone for Marie as she said those words, and exhausted with the effort, closed her eyes and drifted off again. Sally could only imagine Guy's reaction to this, but was quite pleased not to be dealing with him again. He was a nutcase in her opinion, totally unhinged and odious.

Fiona phoned back later to tell Sally that Guy stood quite still after Marie spoke to him, clutching the phone so tightly, Fiona thought he would crush it. He turned to Fiona, a malevolent expression pulling his mouth into a tight, thin line, a visible flush rising from his neck up over his face to where his sandy-coloured hair in unruly tufts, met a slightly receding hairline.

'It's a conspiracy,' he said loudly. 'You're all against me. You're all determined to break us up. I knew this would happen as soon as her family got involved, but she belongs to me. We were going to get married and live in Australia.'

'That might be so,' said Fiona calmly, 'but right now, Marie needs specialist care and as she specifically asked you to leave her be, perhaps you should just respect her wishes and go. When she has recovered and her mind is more settled, I am sure she can clarify the situation between you.'

Without saying another word, Guy turned and stomped off to his room, returning a few moments later with Marie's documents and her house key which he threw down on the kitchen table.

'How am I supposed to get into the house to collect my gear?' he whined, all the fight gone out of him.

'Thank you, Guy.' Fiona quickly scooped up the keys and paperwork. 'Now, there is a flight back to Heathrow this evening. My son, Jamie, will drive you to the airport and make sure you get away safely. You will be met at Marie's house by her other brother, Sean, and his friend who will let you into the house to collect your stuff. The locks are being changed as we speak, so you have no need of the keys.' Fait accompli, thought Fiona, pleased that she, William and Sally had conspired to put all these arrangements in place. Marie would be left in peace now to recover.

*

Sally spent every day of the following two weeks at her mother's bedside only going back in the evening (at Fiona's insistence) to the Westford Guesthouse for a meal, shower and sleep. Marie was in the ICU ward for three days after her operation, then was moved into a rehabilitation ward where she started having regular physiotherapy and speech therapy sessions. They had to be short, as Marie could not stay awake for long, any physical effort completely exhausted her. Sally was horrified the first time the physios got Marie out of bed and helped her to stand, holding on to a Zimmer frame. She was so frail, her once strong and toned arm and leg muscles wasted away, her rib cage and collar bones protruding and visible through the thin material of the hospital gown. She was so unsteady and could not seem to get her legs to work, just shuffling one foot back and forth on the tiled floor. Her damaged brain had lost the ability to send a message to move her leg and feet muscles. It was pitiful to watch and Sally could not believe that her vibrant, active mother had been reduced to this. She was devastated, but bravely hid her shredded emotions from Marie.

Marie would often fall asleep too when Sally was talking to her. Although she appeared to understand what Sally was telling her, she struggled to find the right words to complete a sentence, and tears of frustration would fill her eyes, now mercifully more open with each day that passed. The bruising on her face had faded to a jaundiced-looking yellow, but Sally could not get used to looking at the ghastly scar on Marie's head with its obscene line of vicious- looking black staples. Sally had nightmares about the scar gaping open to reveal Marie's brain tissue, and always had to look away when the nurses came to wash Marie's face and head. After several days, the puckered skin between the staples did not look as livid, but Sally noticed to her horror, that the faint down of hair that was appearing on Marie's shaved scalp was white. Was this a permanent change? How would Marie feel if her rich dark wavy hair was gone for good? She was still young, only forty-three, far too young to have white hair. Sally stopped herself agonizing about this. What did it matter? What mattered was that her mum was alive. Desperately weak and possibly brain damaged, but alive. There was hope and optimism that she could improve, the doctors had said so, hadn't they?

Sally decided to stay positive and to try and stimulate her mother's brain in any way she could. She was a trained dancer and singer after all, she reasoned. She knew how to improve balance and voice projection, she would find a way to modify some of those techniques to help with Marie's recovery further along in the rehabilitation journey.

Just for now, she would observe what the therapists were doing with Marie, and her job would be to keep a reassuring and encouraging presence at her mother's bedside. Marie was still very confused and sometimes could not understand where she was or what had happened to her. Sally would patiently and repeatedly explain that she was in hospital in Johannesburg and that she had undergone brain surgery.

'Mum, you are getting better and in a few more days, the doctors will take out the staples in your head and after that, we are going to stay with Fiona at Westford, her guesthouse, until you are well enough for us to go back home.'

Marie raised her hand to her head and for the first time since the operation, she felt the raised line of the scar that ran all the way from her forehead and halfway across one side of her shaved head. Her eyes opened wide with surprise and shock when she finally realised that her head was shaved and had been cut open.

'Can I see... mirror... Sally please?' Marie looked steadily at Sally, her fingers still feeling the scar on her head.

Sally hesitated. Would the sight of her ravaged head set her mum back? It would be a terrible shock to her, although she reasoned, it might help Marie understand why she felt so weak. 'If you're sure, Mum? Don't get a shock, it still looks bad, but your hair is growing back already…' Oh I shouldn't have mentioned that, she might see it is growing in white. But it was too late now, Marie was determined to look and sat up straighter in her bed while Sally rummaged in her handbag for her mirror. Marie checked the image in the mirror, looked away, checked again.

'Oh my God, is that me? What has happened to me? I look… dreadful!' Tears rolled down Marie's cheeks as, finally, she gazed horrified at her image in the mirror Sally held up in front of her face. 'My hair… is… white.'

'I know, Mum, but it might get darker, but if not then we'll turn you into a ravishing blond!' Sally took the mirror away and smiled at her mum. 'You will look stunning with blond hair and you can wear a fringe to cover the scar. A whole new look for you.' Sally was determined to keep her mum positive. 'But first we will just concentrate on getting you stronger so that we can get out of this hospital and back to Fiona's place. Just wait till you see it, Mum, it's fabulous. I will be sharing a bedroom with you.'

Sally started to describe the large bedroom they

would be sharing but she could see that Marie was exhausted and as soon as she rested her head back on the pillow, her eyes closed and she was asleep. Well this sales pitch on Fiona's house would have to wait for another time when Marie was more alert. Sally was just glad that at least her mum seemed to have grasped that she had an operation. Maybe that would help her to make more sense of why she was so confused and physically weak. If she was honest with herself, Sally was terrified that her mother would never recover properly. Never be the strong, decisive woman she once was. She reflected on the many fierce arguments she had had with her mum in the past, particularly in the years after her dad, Ricky, had just cleared off. Deserted her.

She had adored her charismatic, crazy father. She knew without a doubt that she wanted to be an entertainer like him and had railed against Marie's more pragmatic approach to life. She understood, now that she was older and wiser, that her mum had being trying to protect her from the pitfalls of the lifestyle that had ruined her dad's career. But at the time, when she was desperate to be free of Marie's house rules, she had blamed her mum for her dad's departure; although she had never dared to say that directly to Marie and at times, had hated her mother.

Now as she looked at the pitiful sight of her mum, wasted and bruised, her heart filled with protective compassion and she remembered how hard her mother had worked, three different jobs at times, to support them both. To earn the extra money to pay for Sally to go to college and study performing arts, to support and encourage her in the early days after she graduated and was attending auditions to try and get started in the entertainment industry. She had enjoyed a great career so far, performing in clubs and cabarets, pantomimes, and on cruise ships and had been the lead dancer in a long-running stage show in Cyprus when she got the call from Uncle William about her mum. Well, now it was her turn to look after her mum, however long it took to help her recover, Sally was determined to be there for Marie, to put her own career on hold if need be. There would always be other opportunities for her in the future, her agent would see to that. She was well-known in the entertainment circuit and always in demand.

It was exhausting and draining though. The stress of the past couple of weeks were taking their toll on her nervous system. She could not eat or sleep properly, anxiety gnawed persistently at her mind. Fiona was always offering to relieve Sally of her daily bedside vigil with her mother. Sally occasionally would have to give in and go back to Westford where she would fall into a restless and fear-filled, nightmarish sleep, where she would be trying to run after Guy through thick woods. He was trailing Marie after him and she kept looking back helplessly at Sally, until they disappeared into the impenetrable forest… Sally would come to in a sweat, even in the ceiling-fan coolness of the airy bedroom. Her sheets soaked and crumpled. It was such a relief to wake up and realise that Guy was out of her mother's life, no longer a threat, real or subliminal.

'Mum, the nurse is going to take the staples out of your head now and after the doctor has seen you again tomorrow, we can go back to Fiona's guesthouse. You are doing really well.' Sally squeezed her mum's hand, unable to watch as the nurse carefully removed the hideous black staples which had held Marie's scalp together while the wound healed. It was a noisy process as each staple was clipped apart and dropped with a clang into a metal dish. A few of them missed the dish and bounced on the floor. When the staples were all removed, the nurse gently bathed the scar removing any traces of dried blood left in the indentations of the healing tissue.

Marie had winced as the staples were removed but afterwards seemed pleased to be rid of the pulling sensation on the contracting scar. She ran her hand over her head again, feeling for the scar and the growing soft down of hair that now covered her head.

'Sally, can't go... back... look ugly now.' Marie stared intensely at Sally, struggling to find the words to express her anxiety and discomfort about her appearance. She had always been so proud of her crowning glory, her thick mop of black curls that Ricky had loved to bury his hands into when he kissed her. Images of Ricky kissing her had been a recurring theme in her dreams lately, when she fell into the deep and regular sleeps that punctuated her days and nights in the hospital.

'Look, Mum, I've brought some fabulous scarfs for you to try. What do you think? The colours and designs are lovely, the fabric is really soft and light and Fiona has a whole selection of them at her place. We can tie one round your head, gypsy style. See? Like this lovely blue pattern.' Sally tied the blue scarf round her mum's head and held the mirror up for Marie to see herself.

Marie looked carefully at herself in the mirror, turning her head a little from side to side then pulling the front of the scarf down further over her forehead to hide the scar. 'Your dad... liked me... in blue.'

Sally was puzzled, her mum had rarely mentioned Ricky's name since he disappeared for two years when Sally was sixteen, before he finally sent her a birthday card for her eighteenth, postmarked Sweden. Another two years passed before he included a contact address, inviting Sally to come and visit him. What he hadn't mentioned was that he was living with a woman called Ingrid who had three young children of her own. Despite her initial shocked reaction, Sally had grown to like Ingrid and her children, although she never quite got over the fact that Ricky deserted her to play daddy to another family. It always hurt when she thought about it. Nevertheless, she still adored her father and visited him and his new family in Sweden once or twice a year, in between contracts. Her mum had just shrugged when Sally tried to tell her about her dad's new life.

'Good luck to him,' she would say. 'We were finished a long time ago, I had to get over losing him to drugs, but I can't forgive him for leaving you without a dad. He knew how much you loved him.'

Yet now, here was Marie remembering that blue was Ricky's favourite colour on her. Maybe she had forgotten her troubled past with him? Or maybe she had never really stopped loving him? For years Sally had harboured a secret wish, as children of divorced parents often do, that her mum and dad would get back together, but that was never going to happen. Marie had never wanted to marry again, so why on earth had she got involved with Guy? Was there any truth in Guy's claims that he and her mum were planning on getting married? Surely that was just the ravings of a delusional madman? Sally so wanted that to be the case. She could not stomach the idea of her mum and Guy being together. He was vicious and manipulative, Sally thought, remembering how he had spoken to her before Fiona forced him to leave. Her dad would kill him if he knew what had happened. Sally still could not understand why her mother had been on holiday with Guy, what had she been thinking? Maybe when she was better she would be able to explain.

Fiona, Sally and her Uncle William collected Marie for her journey back to Westford. Sally helped Marie to dress in a short, blue-striped cotton shift dress and tied one of Fiona's donated colourful scarfs round her head. She was pitifully thin and the dress hung off her shoulders, exposing her emaciated limbs. She could shuffle a few steps on a Zimmer frame, but Fiona pushed her in a wheelchair to the car park. Poor Marie was tearful and confused, despite wanting to leave the hospital. She was comforted to be with her family, her much-loved oldest brother, William, Sally and now Fiona, who was a familiar and reassuring presence for Marie. But, going outside into the harsh African sunshine after the subdued light in the ward, filtered through the venetian blinds, left her blinking and shocked at the contrast of light and noise in the busy parking area. The forty-minute drive back to the guesthouse was a nightmare for Marie. Fiona drove as carefully as she could along the motorway. But the roar of passing vehicles travelling much faster than they were, startled Marie, making her feel sick and terrified. Finally, they arrived in the quiet residential suburb of Edenhills and Fiona opened the remote-controlled security gates of her property. Marie could see the smooth driveway leading up to the large house that was Westford, noticed the lush greenery of the palm and fig trees shading the lawns that flanked the driveway and became aware of the heavy, peaceful silence that embraced the air around her. Some of the screeching anxiety beating against her temples subsided a little.

William carried her up the curved stairs and through the open front door into the cool interior of Fiona's home. It would be some time before she ventured unaided up and down those granite stairs.

Marie's recovery was painfully slow and hard for

Fiona, William and Sally to watch. Particularly for Sally, so suddenly thrust into the role of full-time carer for her mum. Marie had always been a strong and capable presence in Sally's life. To see her mother reduced to this childlike, total dependency was heartbreaking and scary for her. Sally had a high-octane personality like her dad Ricky, before her, always on the move, entertaining, performing and used to the limelight. Now she was living life at Marie's pace; helping her to get washed and dressed in the morning took hours at first. Marie would often be so exhausted with the effort that she would fall back onto her bed, washed but back in her dressing gown and unable to eat breakfast until she had another sleep. For the first few days, Fiona would bring a breakfast tray to their bedroom as Sally did not dare leave Marie asleep in case she woke up alone. Marie was still very confused and highly anxious if she could not see a familiar face when she opened her eyes. One of the doctors, several weeks later during a follow-up visit to the hospital, had diagnosed Marie as suffering from post-traumatic stress disorder.

It was always close to midday before Sally could help Marie out of their room in the main part of the house on the same level as the lounge and kitchen, all overlooking the gardens and swimming pool. With

Sally guiding her, they managed to make the short walk to the lounge. Marie would sink into one of the comfortable armchairs underneath the lazily turning ceiling fan which shifted the air and kept her cool. From this position she could see out into the garden and watch Fiona bustling about in and out of the dining room. The other guests would say 'hello' as they passed by, but Sally was always close just in case Marie needed help or reassurance, as she frequently cried and panicked if she woke up after dozing in the armchair. She could not articulate what thoughts were flying across her traumatised brain. Nameless fears arising from past experiences weaving in and out of her damaged memory bank and causing her to shake and try to stand up, to move away from whatever was haunting her. Sally dealt with all of this stoically, but she was struggling not to show her frustration which would bubble up at times when Marie was constantly panicking and Sally had to be the one to calm her down.

Marie responded well when Fiona and William were around her too. She seemed to need the reassurance of the three most familiar faces in her new reality. William was able to set up a temporary office on Fiona's balcony and continue working. His company had a branch office in Johannesburg and occasionally he would leave to spend the working day in town, but was comfortable leaving Marie in the care of Sally and Fiona. He was getting worried about Sally, she had been at her mother's side constantly since she arrived at the hospital and the strain was beginning to show. Sally now had tired blue circles underneath her eyes which seemed too large for the rest of her small facial features and she had lost much of the firm muscle tone that had defined her shapely, petite frame, as she was used to dancing and exercising every day and night during her theatre performances.

William had a word with Fiona. 'Is there any way we can persuade Sally to take a break from caring for Marie? I could pay for a professional carer to come in to help her…' Before he could finish the sentence, Fiona interrupted him.

'No way, William.' She sounded quite fierce. 'Graham and I will take turns to be with Marie so that Sally can have a break. She and my boy, Jamie, seem to have hit it off. I'll get him to persuade Sally to go out with him and meet some other young people her age. Marie is comfortable with us now. We can manage it, don't worry.'

'That would be great, if you are sure Fiona. I will spend as much time with Marie as possible, but I need to put in the hours on this contract I am working on for my company. The travel insurance company require a lot of details and a full report about Marie's operation and ongoing rehabilitation programme, so I am working on that too. I will stay as long as possible, but I must get back to my lovely wife, Moni. I'm missing her and I know she'll be worried about me.' William was sounding stressed too.

'Of course you must miss your wife, William. Sally said Marie managed to walk into the bathroom unaided this morning, so she is improving.' Fiona took William's arm and moved him well out of earshot. 'Look, William, I could do with your advice. I have been trying to protect all of you from something, particularly Marie.' She took a breath. 'Guy has been phoning every day demanding to speak to Marie and now he has started screaming obscenities at me and threatening all of us with 'consequences' for deliberately splitting up him and Marie. He says he is the only one who can help her to recover as he has vital information about what happened to her in Lamu Island. To be honest I don't know how to get him to stop. He has written letters to Marie as well. I still have them.' Fiona spilled all of this out in an agitated rush.

'Right, thanks for telling me, Fiona, and for trying

to protect us, but you let me deal with Guy from now on. You shouldn't have to put up with harassment like that. I'm so sorry, sounds like he has flipped.'

An hour later the phone in the entrance hall rang and as soon as Fiona heard Guy's voice demanding to speak to Marie, she handed the phone straight over to William.

William explained calmly and firmly that Marie was still very unwell and needed to be left in peace to recover. 'Let me have your email address and I will keep you informed about Marie's progress. There will be no more phone calls.'

Fiona had to admire the logical and assertive way William dealt with Guy who must have realised that William was not to be intimidated or manipulated. The phone calls stopped, but William was deluged with daily emails asking about Marie and when she was going home. He answered them with terse one-liners until eventually the emails stopped too.

Marie was making small improvements each day in the run up to Christmas and could manage to walk unaided but very unsteadily, rolling from side to side like a toddler taking its first steps. She was still anxious and confused and would become tearful when she tried some simple task, such as trying to coordinate using a knife and fork, and failed. She could not really understand what had happened to her and why she could not make her body respond the way it used to.

With enormous patience, Fiona would try to involve her in some of the Christmas activities to help stimulate her mind and memory. Marie was able to pick up the baubles for the huge Christmas tree in the lounge that Fiona and Graham were decorating. Her inability to retain any information for more than a moment or two was one of the biggest stumbling blocks for Sally and Fiona, but they kept going, repeatedly giving simple instructions and often having to wait until Marie woke up after falling asleep. The slightest effort, physical or mental, still exhausted her and she struggled to find the right word to complete a sentence. She was terrified of the stairs and could not figure out how to go up or down them. Fiona had to push her in a wheelchair out to her car, through a back entrance with a flat walkway, to the car port, when they had a follow-up hospital appointment.

The neurologist was very pleased and surprised at Marie's progress. He told William and Sally that after such a prolonged and catastrophic brain bleed, he had expected her to permanently lose more functionality.

'Whatever you are doing to rehabilitate her is working, so please carry on. However, it will be some time yet before she is fit to travel. Her brain still needs more recovery time.'

Marie sat at the large table set out for Christmas lunch, surrounded by the now familiar and much-loved faces of Sally, William, Fiona, her husband Graham, and their son and daughter, Jamie and Morgan. A few of Fiona's international house guests who couldn't make it home to their families for the holiday season due to their work commitments in Johannesburg were there too, along with grandparents and a handful of close friends and neighbours. All had met and helped with Marie's rehabilitation. Everyone was welcome to join in the family gathering. It was a noisy, friendly meal with much laughter. She remembered how she always loved the noisy Christmas gatherings with the large extended family of aunts, uncles and cousins she had grown up with and shared family holidays with.

Sally had told Fiona about their usual family festivities and Fiona had created a traditional Christmas lunch to help Marie feel more at home and more normal. Fiona usually served cold cuts of different meats, seafood and endless plates of different salads as it was too hot to eat warm food, even at Christmas. But for this special meal to celebrate Marie's survival, Fiona had sourced all the ingredients of a traditional British Christmas lunch and served roast turkey with all the trimmings and even managed to find Brussels sprouts. Marie ate all of it with relish, the first time she had managed to finish all the food on her plate since she arrived at Westford. Some of the other guests looked bemused at the unusual food combinations on their plates but were soon wolfing it down with evident enjoyment. Fiona had made a huge sherry trifle and even produced a Christmas pudding, flaming blue with brandy, which had Marie clapping her hands in delight and laughing. Only Fiona noticed Marie clutching her head afterwards as if afraid that her new scar would burst open.

She did not show Marie or her family the Christmas card that had arrived for Marie from Queensland, Australia the previous day. She knew it would be from Guy. She would give it to William and let him decide what to do with it. He returned it to the sender without opening it.

5

Marie

I think it was when I was sitting at Fiona's beautifully laid Christmas lunch table that I felt the first stirrings of peace and contentment. From that moment on Lamu Island when the searing, gripping pain in my head possessed me and robbed me of choice, I was drowning in a sea of fear and confusion. I knew I was desperate to get away from Guy, and for someone I trusted to help me understand what was happening to me. I looked at the animated faces of my brother, William, and my dear daughter, Sally, as Fiona brought in the huge turkey and ceremoniously placed it in front of her husband, Graham, for him to carve. It was reminiscent of the celebrations we had at home with my large extended family and for the first time, I felt the fog lifting from my brain and a real connection to my reality, my sense of self.

With all the excitement of the day, I was worn out. Fiona could see I was tiring quickly, it was way past my usual bedtime of 8.30pm. She led me to my room and gave me my medication. Once I was settled, she returned to her guests. I must have fallen asleep within seconds! The next morning I awoke feeling as if I had been to the most wonderful party where I had danced all night. It was such a lovely dream. Then it hit me. I had actually remembered something! My short-term memory had been non-existent since the bleed. I was thrilled and for the first time felt that I might eventually get my life back.

*

Soon after Christmas, my brother William had to return to the UK. He hadn't seen his wife in weeks and his workload was steadily increasing. I sobbed and sobbed when he left and missed him dreadfully. Before leaving, he left instructions with Fiona for my rehabilitation. I was to wash and dress every morning, no matter how long it would take me. He told her he would call every day to speak to me so I could tell him how my day had been. As I couldn't remember anything I had done from one second to the next, he encouraged me to keep a diary of what I had achieved each day. He knew this would be a challenge as the concentration of writing just one short sentence would knock me out and I'd need to sleep for an hour before I was able to write another sentence. Clever William. He knew that if I had promised him, I would keep to it. It meant I'd be working towards my rehabilitation without even realising. I looked forward to his calls, they became the focus of my day and I was excited when I heard the guesthouse phone ring - would it be Will for me? I would hurry in my lopsided way to get to the phone. On good days I would be ready and waiting all day by the phone. On bad days I struggled to keep my eyes open for any length of time, let alone to write, but I still made it to the phone with my notepad to read the three words I'd managed to write that day. Dressed. Sandwich. Garden.

My surroundings were becoming more familiar to me as the days passed and I grew stronger. I loved the spacious, light and airy room I shared with Sally. The gently whirring ceiling fan keeping the room comfortably cool. The walls were hung with stunning paintings by local artists; African women in their colourful tribal dresses and headwear, animals; giraffes, elephants, lions and exotic jungle birds. My least favourite, a witchdoctor performing a tribal dance, his face a scary mask of nose bones, painted stripes and feathers. I particularly liked looking at the picture of an African sunset, the single iconic Baobab tree with its flat canopy of leaves, silhouetted against a huge orange sun, the surrounding sky splashed in deep orange, amber and pink swathes. I found that image very soothing when I woke up suddenly from one of my endless naps in the early days of my stay at Westford.

Sally was never far from me at first and I know I was leaning heavily on her, literally and metaphorically, for my survival. It must have been a huge strain on her, but she was incredibly patient as I struggled to achieve all the simple tasks of looking after myself. I simply could not remember or work out how to do things and I know that my efforts often ended in angry, frustrated tears. But oh, the joy I felt the first time I managed to write my own name after many days of trying. It was such an achievement for me, and all the family and guests stood around congratulating me. I felt as if I had won a marathon to be so supported and encouraged by everyone living in Westford. They were behaving just like my large family back home. I was pleased when Sally felt comfortable enough to leave me, and started going out socialising with Fiona's son, Jamie. There was always someone nearby, Fiona, Graham, or one of the guests who would materialize at my side to help or guide me if I appeared to be struggling. I was mesmerized by the view from my bedroom into the garden but at first, I could not manage to negotiate the few steps that led out into the garden from the lounge. I had an irrational fear of steps and stairs. One day as I stood hesitating at the steps, desperate to take a walk and explore the garden, Fiona appeared beside me.

'Would you like to take a wee walk round the garden, Marie? The agapanthuses are in full bloom, they look amazing. I'd love to show them off to you. I grew them all from seed.'

How strange that Fiona mentioned agapanthus. I had them in my garden at home. I remembered that. Ricky bought the original plant for me years ago, soon after we moved to our new house. He said the blue of the flowers reminded him of the colour of my eyes.

I held tightly onto Fiona's arm and slowly, slowly, I walked sideways down the few steps into the garden. I was delighted with myself and Fiona led me to a bench under the shade of a broad-leaved fig tree to rest for a few moments. We continued, slowly walking around Fiona's wonderful garden that she had cultivated herself over the years, from reduced price, end-of-season plants bought from the market stalls. She must have green fingers, I thought. I have never seen such a profusion of lush plants, grasses, shrubs and cacti, all surprisingly mixed and matched in random groups that gave the garden an air of mystery and serenity. Desert cacti and pampas grasses rose majestically over beds of delphiniums and roses. A few steps further and my senses were assailed with the sight and scent of pure white jasmine blossom mixed with the sharper tang of a lemon tree also in full bloom, with blood-red poinsettias contrasting and crowding the borders. Every bed we passed, holding both exotic shrubs and flowers I could not name, blending in harmony with the familiar shapes and scents of carnations and geraniums, was a delight. I was enthralled. My brain sang with the joy of feeling so at peace for the first time in months.

Another surprise greeted me as we rounded a curve in the garden. There in the middle of a small pond overhung with the drooping branches of willow trees, danced a triumphant, full-sized Zulu warrior, sculpted from a huge rock pitted with sparkles of fool's gold, that had been brought out of a gold mine, Fiona told me later. There he was, frozen in time, arms lifted in triumph, one leg bent and raised in dance, but what made me laugh out loud with delight, was the surprised and happy expression on his face, his eyes turned downwards, peering down his nose, to watch in eternal amazement as water gushed from his open mouth, pouring down his glistening bare chest and splashing brightly into the pond. I could see the shadows of enormous gold fish criss-crossing under the bubbling disturbance. The sound of my own laughter took me by surprise too. I had forgotten what it felt like to feel happy and delighted with life. Fiona laughed with me, or perhaps she was crying, it was hard to tell. Together we walked slowly back to the house.

Every day after that, I would take a stroll, supported by a walking stick, round Fiona's magical gardens. At first, someone always came with me or at least helped me up and down the stairs. It was usually one or other of the guests and I became quite friendly with a few of them. I always stopped and sat on the bench near the stone Zulu warrior and knew that, slowly, I was healing, letting go of the fear and trauma that had dominated my mind for months. Sometimes when we were back at the hospital for one of my many follow-up appointments, I would catch a glimpse of someone who looked like Guy. Often just the back of a head or a gesture would startle me and restimulate my anxiety.

Invariably I would then have the recurring nightmare of being pursued by him, my feet sinking into sticky mud as he drew closer and closer…

At last I was told I was fit enough to fly home to the UK. The insurance company arranged for a nurse to fly out from England to accompany Sally and me back. The nurse, a pleasant middle-aged chap called Martin, arrived the night before our departure and was clearly bemused to be drawn into the lively impromptu party that had spilled out from the dining room onto the covered patio overlooking the gardens. All Fiona's guests stayed on after dinner to join us in a farewell drink. Everyone hugged and kissed me and Sally as if we were loved family members and wished us good luck. It was an amazing, unforgettable evening. At some time every day, Fiona would be playing a Miriam Makeba album and I too fell in love with the wonderful voice of this South African soul and jazz singer, Mama Africa, exiled from her homeland for her stand against apartheid. I was already familiar with her voice; she was one of Ricky's best-loved singers. That last evening, Fiona played my two favourite tracks, *Malaika*, Swahili for "*I love you my angel*" which reduced me to tears, and the livelier *Pata Pata* dance song that many of the guests jigged about to, collapsing in hysterics as they tried to copy the

Zhosa tribal click, part of the various vocabularies that Miriam had made famous in her recordings.

Sally and I had been living with Fiona and Graham for almost three months, treated and cherished by them as if we were part of the family. They had supported and cared for me and Sally during the worst time of my life and I doubted, from what I knew of my time in hospital, if I would have survived without her intervention. The prospect of going back to my old life in England terrified me. All my needs were taken care of here at Westford. I did not have to make any decisions, apart from choosing what to wear each day from the selection Sally would lay out on the bed while I was showering. I was never left alone for long here, help was always at hand. How would I manage back home? My brain ached trying to think about it.

We had to leave just after dawn for the journey to Johannesburg International Airport. I had not expected to see the guests so early in the morning as we had said our farewells the night before. But there they were, assembled on the front steps, sleepy-eyed, most still in their nightclothes watching me being wheelchaired round the side of the house to the waiting car. There were more tears and hugs all round before we finally pulled out of the drive to start the long journey back home to continue my recovery. Sally and I both cried in the car most of the way to the airport. My last sight of South Africa before we entered the anonymity of the airport, was a group of young Zulu men singing acapella style, a triumphant tribal chorus, as they waited for transport to pick them up for their week's work at the mines.

The airport lights were dazzlingly bright. The lights and fast paced hustle and bustle of airport life was too much for me. The past few months had been calm, quiet and moving at a pace I could manage. My eyes darted from side to side trying to keep focus on people and trolleys whizzing by me. I covered my ears to block out the noise. Martin put a blanket over my head to shield me from the bright lights and the check-in girl guided us to a quiet private lounge to wait for our flight.

I don't remember much about the flight home, Sally was still tearful, having had to say goodbye to Jamie. They were in a full-on relationship by then. The insurance company had paid for us to fly back in 1st class. It was luxury. We each had a separate compartment with a bed, slippers and a filled wash bag. Martin fussed around me making sure I was comfortable and settled, but I must have dropped off almost immediately. I was vaguely aware of Martin checking my temperature and blood pressure at intervals during the flight, but I could not stay awake for long.

*

My youngest brother, Sean, collected us from Heathrow. He was a chauffeur for a wealthy businessman, so we rode home in style in his boss's limousine. I could see that Sean was shocked at my changed appearance. The last time he had seen me I was a curvaceous brunette with long curly hair. I must have looked dreadful to him, all skinny limbs, a livid scar on my forehead, still showing under the warm winter wool beanie that Sally made me wear for our arrival back into the chill of an English winter.

'Oh, sis. We thought we were going to lose you…' Sean, who did not have a sentimental bone in his body was holding me tightly, his voice cracking up with emotion. He quickly sniffed and got all brusque. 'C'mon let's get you home. All the family have been there sorting the house out and cooking up a storm, so you and Sal can just relax and get over the jet lag.'

There was a welcome committee waiting for us. All my aunts, uncles and cousins were indoors, it was too cold to stand outside. It was a bit overwhelming for me to be honest. By the time I had been

137

embraced by everyone, I was exhausted. Poor Martin was hugged and kissed as well. That's my exuberant family for you.

'Marie needs to rest now,' he told them firmly and ushered everyone out, except Aunt Doreen, who refused to budge and declared that she would be staying to look after us for a day or two. I was so grateful to hear that, I was incapable of doing anything remotely logical at this stage and Sally too, was utterly spent.

*

I hardly recognised my own home. It seemed so small and dark after spending many weeks in Fiona's spacious lodge home where every room hummed and shimmered with translucent African light.

I had left for a Kenyan safari treat with Guy, confident, capable but exhausted. Content enough with my busy life. I came back to an altered reality with an eight-inch scar on my head, barely concealed under a short mop of white hair, still experiencing anxiety attacks when memories of Guy's insane behaviour were triggered by glimpses of men who resembled him.

Who was this person staring back at me from my full-length bedroom mirror?

'Don't worry about how you look, Mum, you are still recovering.' Sally tried to lead me away from the startling reflection in the mirror.

I rarely looked at myself in Fiona's mirrors. I was always too tired to concentrate or care how I looked then. I pulled away from Sally and continued to stare at the person gazing back at me with huge, dark blue sunken eyes. Yes, it was me, but I was horrified at how I looked now. My complexion was sallow, the skin dry and lifeless. A deep line ran between my eyes, entrenched from weeks of frowning against the pain in my head. I was so skinny! I was always wanting to be a bit thinner but this pathetic creature staring back at me was almost skeletal, clothes hanging loosely from my shoulders and hips. The white hair and the livid scar showing through made me look like an old woman. My lovely shiny dark hair, my pride and joy, if I'm honest, all gone. I could not help it, tears of self-pity welled up and spilled unchecked over my cheeks. My nose filled up just as quickly and joined in the cascade.

'Mum, oh, Mum. Please don't cry.' Sally materialised bedside me, tissues in hand and drew me gently away to sit on the bed. We sat like that for a while as she rocked me in her arms, just as I once did for her. 'I am going to fatten you up with lots of potatoes, pasta and rice, Mum.' Sally said lightly after my tears stopped flowing. 'How about changing your look altogether and becoming a ravishing blond? They always say blonds have more fun, don't they?'

Sally took my hand away from where I had been unconsciously rubbing the deep line between my eyes. 'Nothing that a bit of collagen filler or Botox can't sort out, Mum. Many people in the entertainment business, including the men, do that all the time. You will soon be beautiful again, Mum, I promise you.'

Dear Sally, she had been my rock for weeks, giving up her job to help take care of me in Johannesburg and now, determined to stay at home with me until I was stronger and could be independent again. I owed it to her to get better as quickly as I could. I could not bear for her to sacrifice her own life and ambitions to be my carer. I knew I had a struggle ahead of me. I could barely walk more than a few wobbly steps, like a toddler, Sally said, before having to sit down, exhausted. I was still afraid of walking upstairs, although I could not understand why and did not tell Sally as it seemed so irrational. I think she knew though as she always appeared whenever I made a move to go upstairs, citing some reason why she was going upstairs too.

My worst problem was finding the right word to express my thoughts. I always knew in my head what I wanted to say but often the word I needed to make sense of the sentence, slipped out of my brain before it reached my lips. This, more than any other limitation caused me great frustration, often making me cry sorry-for-myself tears which I could not control. Poor Sally, she handled all my weird behaviour with great patience. She must have warned my brothers, aunts and friends who came to the house to help, what to expect, as everyone was good at completing my sentences for me. Sometimes they guessed wrong but that would make me laugh, better than their helpless looks if I ended up weeping and angry.

Thank God for my family and friends though, it was the only time Sally would leave me to go out with her crowd, for a change of scene. I am sure she was missing Jamie too. They had grown very close in Johannesburg and they were on the phone together almost every day. Sally took care of paying all the bills from my account. I did not care what the phone was costing. She deserved it. I rarely answered the phone at first when we arrived home as I could barely string a sentence together and usually the calls were for Sally from Jamie.

I heard her voice raised in anger one day. I was in

the downstairs loo and could not hear what she was saying. When I came out she was still standing by the phone in the hallway with her fists clenched and red splotches flushing her normally creamy complexion.

'Who was that, Sally?' I managed to say before staggering back into the lounge and collapsing onto the sofa, exhausted once again. 'You sounded angry and upset. You didn't have an argument with Jamie, did you?'

'Mum, I don't know if I should tell you this but…' she hesitated, a frown furrowing her forehead.

'What Sally, what? Tell me!'

'It was Guy, Mum. He was demanding to speak to you. He said he was the only one who could help you get better - said you loved each other and should be together! I'm sorry, Mum, I told him to eff off and not to call again. He is such a dick. I can't bear him!' Sally's voice rose an octave.

My stomach cramped immediately. My heart beat wildly. My throat constricted. The place where my scar scored my head throbbed in sudden painful spasm. 'Oh no, Sally. I can't believe…' I could not find the words to finish but I could not believe that Guy was still trying to get in touch with me after being told so often when he tried that tactic in Johannesburg, that I did not want to see him or speak to him again. What was wrong with him? He must be completely bonkers if he really believed that we were ever a serious item. Surely, I never said or did anything to make him think that? How I wished I had not given in and slept with him before we left for Kenya. Where was he now? Had he phoned from Australia or was he back in England? He knows where I live of course... my mind went into overdrive.

The phone calls continued after that with terrifying regularity. If Sally answered, as she always did when she was at home, he would hang up as soon as he heard her voice. Sometimes when I picked up the phone and spoke, he would rush out a few words before I could hang up.

'Marie, Marie, please. I need to see you...'

'Leave me alone, Guy, or I will call the police.' I said that to him the first few times and then after that, I would just slam the phone down without saying anything. But I was always shaking and angry afterwards.

It was unusual for anyone to come to the front door. All my regular visitors would come in through the kitchen door as that was closest to my parking spaces. The knocking at the front door one evening was loud and persistent. Ricky had never found the time to fix the bell and I had not bothered either. Sally opened the door. I was a few feet behind her in the hallway. Guy was sandwiched between two burly policemen, glaring red-faced at Sally as she blocked the doorway.

'Sorry to disturb you miss, but this gentleman claims that a Mrs White at this address, has unlawful possession of some jewellery belonging to him.' The policeman was looking at me over Sally's diminutive frame. Guy was now staring straight at me, his pale-blue eyes blinking and intense.

I didn't hesitate, despite the shock of seeing him at close quarters again. 'Yes, I have a gold cross he gave me. He said it belonged to his mother. I'll give it back. Wait.' I tried not to show my alarm at seeing him turn up on my doorstep. My reaction was visceral as my stomach cramped and my palms turned slick with sweat. Fortunately, the gold cross and chain were in a drawer in the sideboard downstairs, where I kept some pieces of jewellery I rarely wore. I was not moving well, my steps more unsteady than usual. Sally stepped back, took the cross and chain from me and thrust it into Guy's hand. He shoved it into his pocket and tried to take a step forward into the hallway.

'Is this all you wanted to recover, sir?' The policeman placed his hand firmly over Guy's elbow and raised his eyebrows apologetically at Sally and me. Guy had the grace to look embarrassed.

'Yes,' Guy muttered. 'It belonged to my mother, it's all I have left of hers now.'

I recognised that poor-me whine in his voice that he had often used when we were clearing out his dad's house. It was a well-practiced technique of his to get sympathy. It made me cringe now. He must have been hoping for a reaction from me, maybe hoping he could gain access to the house if I had protested.

The policemen were not impressed. 'I trust this gentleman will have no further reason to disturb you madam,' one of them said, pointedly looking at Guy who was staring intently at me. Still holding him by the elbow, they steered him down the step at my front door.

Sally stood with her back against the closed door. 'Can you believe that creep, Mum? What is he on? I hope he gets told off for wasting police time!'

I could only hope that was the last I would see of him. But I was badly shaken. What was he doing back here in the UK? My nightmares started again.

My recovery was slow and steady. I had regular sessions with the physiotherapist and occupational therapist to help me co-ordinate my balance and re-learn how to complete simple tasks around the house. Making myself a cup of tea was a great triumph and made me feel that I was getting my control back. Ricky always used to tease me about my fussy ritual with tea drinking. I always insisted on brewing it in a teapot before drinking it out of a china cup and saucer. No mugs for me. I made a total mess of it the first few times I tried. The tea went everywhere. But persistence won and soon I was successfully making myself cups of tea several times a day - just because I could. Gradually my brain-fog began to lift and I was concentrating for longer without falling asleep after the smallest effort. A mobile hairdresser came when my scar was almost covered by my new growth of white hair. I hated it. I couldn't go back to being a brunette, I would have had an endless battle with my white roots. Not a good look. The hairdresser transformed me into a strawberry blond which suited my complexion and seemed to make my eyes shine with renewed life. I was quite taken with my new look and felt more confident about my appearance. I just needed to practice walking, I was still stumbling along a bit indoors but needed to start building my confidence walking outside. At first, Sally came with me and let me hold her arm as I carefully negotiated the cracks and bumps in the uneven pavement near my house. Eventually, I felt confident enough to try walking on my own and every day I would walk the short length of my road to the corner and back again. It would take all my concentration and energy to achieve this and I would need to rest for an hour when I made it back to the house. But I was determined and so pleased with myself for managing.

One day, I was about halfway to the corner when I looked up and saw him walking quickly towards me. Oh my God! Guy was bearing down on me, a beaming smile splitting his face. I panicked and tried to side-step him, but he stopped right in front of me blocking my path. I side-stepped again. He blocked me.

'Marie, darling. How are you? I've missed you so much. They wouldn't let me see you. But I'm here now. I will help you recover.' He tried to embrace me. I pushed him away. He was so big, standing there looming over me. 'You're just a bit upset. Please let's go back to the house. I'll make you a cup of tea, just the way you like it. Or we can go somewhere and talk everything through. You know I will take care of you.'

'Guy, leave me alone. I don't want to see you

again. Just go away!' My voice was shrill and I knew that I had wet myself.

'Don't be silly, Marie. We love each other. I am here to help you. I've rented a flat down the road. You are all I have now.' His voice dropped into his whine tone and he tried to take hold of my arm.

I must have looked frightened because a car pulled up alongside us and a woman rolled down her window.

'Are you all right, love? Do you need any help?'

I shook Guy's hand off my arm and replied to the woman. 'Thanks, it's OK. He is just leaving. My house is nearby.' I glared at Guy. 'Just go!'

Guy's face turned red and his lips thinned. He narrowed his eyes and stared at me for a long moment. The woman in the car did not move. He left.

I don't know how I made it home, but somehow, I got through the door and collapsed, shaking and crying with the shock. He had said he was renting a flat nearby. Could that be true? Was he going to be stalking me now? I didn't know what to do. Should I tell the police? My brain could not cope and I fell into a fretful sleep, punctuated with my recurring nightmare of Guy, pursuing me through boggy marshland that sucked at my feet until my legs were trapped and I could run no further.

I woke up in a sweat, in time to hear the phone ringing. Sally had just walked in and was talking quickly and quietly to someone. 'I'll need to ask Mum.' I heard her say. What now? I was beyond being capable of passing an opinion on anything.

'Mum, it's Jamie, he is ready to leave Johannesburg now, and booked his flight. Are you still sure we can stay here with you until we find a place of our own?' Sally's eyes were shining with excitement.

I had told Fiona that Jamie was welcome to come and stay with me anytime as it was obvious that our children were in love. At least something wonderful had come out of my near-death experience in South Africa. Fiona had been so unbelievably kind to me and Sally in Johannesburg. Looking after us like we were family. I honestly think I might have died had it not been for Fiona's dedicated care of me in the early days before I had my operation.

I didn't tell Sally about my scary encounter with Guy. I did not want to worry her. She was so happy that her Jamie was finally coming to be with her. He arrived a few days later and the daily phone calls from Guy stopped soon after that. Jamie would answer the phone for us which probably scared Guy off, as he realised there was a man in the house now. I began to feel safer with both Sally and Jamie living with me and resumed my practice walks up and down the street. Perhaps Guy had finally got the message?

Then the letter arrived. It was from Guy, demanding that I paid him back £3000, the money he said he lost cancelling the safari trip in Kenya. I ignored it until the insurance company contacted me. They said my "husband" was trying to claim money for the expenses he had incurred because of my operation. I was furious and told them not to have any further communication with him. He was *not* my husband and this was a fraudulent claim. That must have scared him off too because he went quiet after that. Except a month or two later, on July 4th, I remembered the date as it was Independence Day in the USA. I picked up the phone and all I could hear was someone breathing. There was no reply when I said 'hello'. Immediately my skin crawled and I quickly replaced the receiver. I was sure it was Guy, but when I dialled 1471 to retrieve the number, it had been withheld. It was a few days before I made a possible connection. Guy's birthday was on July 4th. I was helping him sort out his dad's house after the funeral. It was a few days before July 4th.

'It's my birthday soon,' he announced mournfully, 'but now that I am an orphan,' (he did say that) 'I don't suppose I will even get a card. I'm all alone in the world now.' His eyes filled with tears yet again.

I did feel sorry for him, he had no relatives now, (apart from my departed ex, his much loathed cousin, Ricky) so when I got back home, I quickly put together a small package of a few treats for him; sweets, a small bottle of wine and a card and sent it to his dad's cottage. He called me the night of his birthday when I got home from work.

'Oh, Marie, thank you so much for the card and the present! You have no idea how much that means to me. You are the only person who cares about me now that Dad has gone.' His effusive tone changed when he mentioned his dad and I just knew that he would be wiping tears away as he always did whenever he spoke about his father. Odd really that he was so upset. He and his dad had never had a good relationship. Maybe he was mourning what he wished it might have been…

With hindsight, I realised what a prime manipulator and controller he was. He made me feel sorry for him and I let him into my home, and eventually my bed. He had behaved well for the weeks before we went on holiday together, but I remember all the little insidious controlling incidents that should have made me more suspicious of the dark character lurking beneath the outward charm. He was always questioning me about my motives for doing certain things and suggesting that I change my habits. Offering what he said were better solutions. I was only faintly irritated about him moving my furniture around and rearranging my kitchen cupboards. At the time, after an exhausting day at work and often visiting my mother on the way home, it was marvellous to come home to a cooked meal and some convivial company.

He had scared me the last night in my bedroom, before we left for Kenya. He produced his hunting knife from under the pillow and jokingly ran the tip of it down the inside of my arm, raising the lightest trail of scratched skin. He laughed when I pulled my arm away.

'Better not take this baby on a safari holiday. I could take down a lion with this knife, it's so sharp.'

'You're crazy, Guy,' I said lightly, but my heart was pounding. 'You gave me a fright. That knife is lethal. Put it away for God's sake.'

'Sorry, Marie. I didn't mean to frighten you. It's all

I have left to remind me of Dad…' I knew that tone by then. He was just about to cry. I pulled him close and kissed him. It was easier than consoling him through another emotional tsunami.

The first time I saw the knife was when I drove him to Virginia Water in Surrey to scatter his father's ashes. He said that was his dad's favourite place to go walking with his mum. We went mid-week when it was quiet and he scattered the ashes at the water's edge when nobody was around. I wasn't sure if we could do that or not and I kept looking around nervously in case anyone saw us. We started walking back along the path, when Guy suddenly produced this huge knife and proceeded to carve initials into the trunk of an ancient oak, his knife biting deeply into the thick, gnarled wood

'Guy! Stop! You can't do that here. These trees are protected!' I was horrified.

'Strike me flaming roan, Marie! I want to carve my dad's initials near his ashes. What's wrong with that?' Guy's voice was loud and high in protest. An older couple suddenly appeared around the corner of the lakeside pathway and saw this large, red-faced Australian fellow brandishing a huge knife. They looked at us in horror and almost sprinted past, not even looking back to see if I was still uncarved. Guy walked behind me back to the car, grumping about how uptight we Brits were. By the time I drove back to my house, he had regained his composure and I did not see the ghastly knife until he produced it again from under the pillow. Did he sleep with it in his own bed?

How easily he had fooled Fiona too, at first. She had felt sorry for him as he had acted so helplessly emotional when she first encountered him at the hospital in Johannesburg and had invited him back to her guesthouse. The other guests had also felt sorry for him as he spun his web of lies around them all, telling them that he had no money left and was so desperately worried about his poor wife. They all bought him drinks at the bar and Fiona thinks that one or two of them might have given him money.

It was months before I began to feel completely safe again, and having Jamie living with Sally and me certainly helped to make me feel more secure. There was no more contact from Guy and I had no idea where he was. Just hoping that he had returned to his life in Australia and had given up on his wild fantasy about him and me being in a relationship. Except, the next year when July 4th came around, I received another silent phone call with a withheld number. I could never be sure of course, but this became an annual event which always unsettled me.

Some other conversations I had about Guy with some of his dad's old friends and neighbours just reinforced what a conman he was at heart. They must have heard what had happened to me, probably from my Aunt Doreen who was a great gossip and kept in touch with everyone who had a remote connection to the family. Of course, they wanted to know how I was recovering but the conversation soon turned to them having a moan about Guy, saying what a sponger he was and that he had been in touch with them after his dad's funeral asking if they would store his dad's furniture in their garage until he decided what pieces he wanted to keep and could he possibly stay with them? All to save money on hiring a storage unit and a hotel bed. They refused.

Sean, my younger brother, also told me that when they had met Guy at my house after changing the locks, they followed him into every room, watching him collect his stuff and making sure he did not touch anything of mine. Sean said Guy was furious, all red in the face and puffing, stomping through each room, stuffing his things into a rucksack. In the spare room where most of his clothes were, he pulled out the drawer of the small cabinet and out came the large hunting knife. Sean said, for a moment he and his mate nearly wet themselves with fright as Guy wheeled round clutching his knife and glared at them, before shoving it into his rucksack pocket without saying a word.

'He is a seriously weird dude, sis. He had better stay well away from you.'

*

I was making good progress and after a year of intensive rehabilitation at home, I was considered fit enough to return to work. My bank had kept my job open for me and at first, I would take a taxi in and stay for two hours, three days a week. But I had to relearn everything! I could not even remember how to turn on my computer. My colleagues were very patient with me and gradually my skills returned. But oh, I tired so quickly and had to take frequent naps at work; sometimes at my desk. Eventually, I increased my office hours and the joyful day came when I got my driving licence back and I could live independently again.

Sally was getting restless and I sensed that the relationship with Jamie was floundering. They were very different in character. He was quiet, conservative and cautious, while Sally was a will o' the wisp, a free spirit, longing for action and adventure.

'Mum, I hope you don't mind, but now that you are so much stronger, I want to sign up for another contract on the cruise liners. They have offered one to me, leaving this weekend. Working in an office is driving me crazy with boredom.'

I was half expecting this. 'What about Jamie, will he keep?'

'I think you know already, Mum. Jamie's great, but I can't make my future with him. It's time for me to move on. Jamie is happy to stay living here with you. He can help keep crazy Guy at bay.'

Jamie was quiet for a while after Sally left, spending a lot of time in his room at first. But it was a relief for me to have someone in the house. The spectre of Guy turning up again was always twitching at my mind. Jamie's solid, unprepossessing presence was a comfort.

Sally's contract lasted for six months. I did miss her. She had been with me every minute during my recovery and I realised how much I had come to depend on her taking charge of all the practical aspects of my life: ordering groceries, paying utility bills, arranging doctor and hospital appointments for me. I had become complacent, thinking that I still needed to be managed. Before she went, she left all my bills up to date and in good order, so it was a week or two before I had to deal with household issues myself. How empowering it was for me to cope with running my life myself! I was on a roll.

*

'Mum, it's Dad. His lung cancer is back. They can't do any more for him. Mum, he's all alone in Sweden now. Please can he come home?'

No! No! I was clutching the phone so hard, my fingers cramped. What was Sally asking me to do? I had not seen Ricky for years since he shot through without saying goodbye. The woman he had lived with for decades had died, ironically, of cancer and now apparently, he was terminally ill too. Sally had kept up her relationship with him and his second family. She still adored her dad and had long ago forgiven him for deserting her. But now, he wanted to come home to me. To us. I was still living in the same house I had shared with him after we married. The same house where Sally was born and where he had mismanaged his life in spectacular form for seventeen years.

How could I say no? Perhaps I had never really stopped loving him. I had simply learned to live without him. I could not bear to think of him dying alone and unloved in some Swedish hospice.

Sally had warned me that he was very thin. But to see my once dark and handsome ex-husband worn away with disease was shocking. The luxuriant dark curls were no more. A few wisps of grey hair clung to his scalp, his eyes were deeply sunk and his cheeks hollowed. Yet, when he smiled at me, I could see a shadow of the old charmer, the charismatic Ricky that could turn any situation into a stand-up routine.

'Thank you for letting me come home, Marie. It won't be for long. I promise. I should have listened to you all those years ago. You always said the fags and booze would kill me…'

Sally and Jamie were great with him when she was in between trips. She was only booking short contracts of a few weeks so she could spend time with him. I wanted to keep him at home until the end if possible, and for a while he seemed to rally and would come and sit downstairs with me and watch some television. We both dozed off all the time, like an old married couple. It wasn't too unpleasant.

The front door bell was working. Jamie had fixed it. Sally and Jamie were upstairs in their respective rooms.

'I'll get it,' said Ricky heaving himself out of the

armchair. He was having quite a good day, but as usual, we had both fallen asleep in front of the nine o'clock news. He shuffled out into the hallway and I followed him. Wondering who was visiting so late on in the evening? Hopefully not the local council candidate on a last-minute push for support at the election the next day.

Ricky opened the front door just as I got to the hallway, still groggy from sleep.

'You! What the fuck!' Guy's bulk filled the doorway. He pushed Ricky aside with one arm. Ricky, too weak to react, stumbled and fell backwards onto the bottom stair. Guy was glaring manically at me, his eyes, glittering slits. I could see spittle on his mouth. The gleam of the hunting knife clutched in his hand, froze the blood in my veins. I opened my mouth to scream. No sound came out.

'You were mine, Marie. You'll always be mine. You said you were finished with him.' Guy gestured at Ricky, struggling to get to his feet.

I was mesmerised by Guy's knife, held high, ready to strike. I could smell the alcohol on his breath. He was going to kill me. My brain was screaming a command to flee. I was paralysed with fear.

It happened in a blur. I saw Ricky raise his arm

behind Guy. He thumped something on the back of Guy's head with a ghastly crack. Guy toppled, sprawled full-length in my hallway, inches from my feet, his head oozing dark red blood onto the beige carpet runner. The knife had slithered out of his grasp and was lying inches from his head. Ricky was leaning heavily against the wall, still clutching the brightly-coloured stone carving of a Zulu chief's head that Fiona had insisted on giving me. Now, forever more, a grisly memento of my time in Johannesburg. It had pride of place on my hall table. Ricky and I were speechless, the adrenalin coursing through our veins robbing us of any coherent action. Ricky was hyperventilating, near to collapsing.

Sally and Jamie came thundering down the stairs. 'Oh my God! What happened? Is he dead?' Sally dropped to her knees beside Guy's inert body, feeling for a pulse. 'He's alive.' Her voice came out in a high squeak.

I heard Jamie's voice. It seemed to be coming from far away. 'Ambulance please. Head injury. Yes. Unconscious, but has a pulse. Yes. Send the police too. Don't touch the knife, Sally! Get your mum and dad out of here.'

The paramedics and the police arrived together.

One of them ducked quickly into the lounge and had a look at me and Ricky, sitting stunned and shaking on the sofa.

'Don't move,' he commanded us. 'I'm calling for back-up.' Within a few minutes, Guy's unconscious body was being stretchered out. I heard the sirens wailing and imagined the blue lights flashing as the ambulance sped off. I was shaking uncontrollably by now, my mind trying to process what had just happened. Ricky was sitting beside me on the sofa, his breathing shallow and laboured. The police officers came into the room and sat opposite us. A man and a woman this time. They wanted statements, but we were incapable of speaking coherently. Sally brought sweet tea in mugs. No china cup and saucer this time. Guy's knife and my Zulu head carving were already in plastic bags. Evidence? Fingerprints? What if they charged Ricky with the attack on Guy? What if Guy died from his head injury? Would Ricky be charged with murder? But it was a defensive attack. Guy was going to kill me. I shuddered as the reality of that sunk in.

Miraculously, from somewhere deep in his ravaged body, Ricky had found the strength to floor Guy with that mighty blow. He had saved my life. All these thoughts were rushing through my head as the police officer was questioning us, trying to piece together what had happened and why. I took Ricky's hand, it was cold and clammy.

'Please,' I managed to say. 'My husband is unwell. Can this wait?'

The police officers stood up. 'Sorry, but I am afraid that you both must accompany us to the police station for further questioning. A serious crime has been committed here.'

'You can't take them now!' Sally shrieked. 'Can't you see they are both in deep shock.' She stood defensively in front of us, trying to shield us.

'Step aside, miss.'

'Sarg?' The female officer was looking doubtfully at her colleague.

'My wife was being threatened, officer. It was me that hit him over the head. I am responsible. I'll come with you willingly.' Ricky tried and failed, to stand up.

The new paramedic, the back-up first responder, appeared and shouldered the police officers aside. Jamie must have opened the front door for him.

'Sorry, mate, I need to check these folks out before they go anywhere. I'm Greg,' he said as he knelt in front of Ricky and me, opening his green satchel, revealing a display of life-saving equipment. 'I would like to check your blood pressure first. You first, sir, please. What's your name?'

The policeman did not leave the room while our vital signs were being checked over. But I heard the female officer talking to Sally and Jamie in the hallway. Sally's voice was high and agitated as she tried to describe what had happened. I heard her use the word 'psycho' a few times.

Finally, the paramedic snapped his bag closed. He stood up and faced the policeman. 'These folks are not fit enough to go to the police station with you now. If you need a statement from them, I will stay with them until you are finished. This gentleman is very unwell and I am calling for an ambulance to take him to hospital.'

The policeman tried to stare him down, but our green-clad saviour was not budging.

Somehow, after another cup of sweet tea, we managed to answer a few questions which had to serve as our preliminary statement, before the second ambulance arrived. The policeman was not happy. I was not happy either. I did not want Ricky to go into hospital. I sensed that he would not recover from the trauma we had just experienced. Yet, it was a better option than being carted off to the police station to answer more questions so late at night.

I wanted to go with him, but Sally would not let me.

'No way, Mum. I'll go with Dad in the ambulance. Jamie will stay with you and I'll get a taxi back once Dad is settled.'

'I'll be staying with you too.' The female officer smiled kindly at me.

Did they think I was a flight risk? I half expected her to ask for my passport.

I managed to have a few words with Ricky before the ambulance left. 'You saved my life, Ricky. Thank you. By the way, you called me your wife.' Odd how that had touched me. We had been divorced for years.

He managed a grin. 'Well, you called me your husband… thanks for letting me come home, Marie. I never stopped loving you. I'm so sorry I screwed up.'

The phone ringing woke me up. I heard the murmur of Jamie's voice in the hallway. I looked at my illuminated bedside clock. 3am. I waited. Jamie knocked softly on my bedroom door and came in.

'Marie, that was Sally. Ricky passed away a few moments ago. She asked me to tell you. She will be on her way home soon.'

I lay quietly, watching the faint shadows of the cloud-covered moon filtering in and out through the gap in the curtains, reflecting with some regret, the years spent apart from Ricky.

Sally crept into the bed beside me. She was cold, shivering, her face wet with tears. Both too exhausted to speak. I put my arms around her and held her till she slept.

*

The police told me that they could not charge Guy with attempted murder as he was in a coma and might not recover. However, if he did and was well enough to stand trial, I would be called as the main prosecution witness to the assault. I was the only witness. Ricky was dead and Sally and Jamie did not actually see what had happened. The defence lawyers could have a field day with that one, I imagined. Fortunately, Fiona, Graham and William, my brother, would be backing up my story of Guy's bizarre behaviour in Johannesburg.

Fiona and Graham had moved back to live in the depths of rural Herefordshire. The unsettled dynamics and political unrest in South Africa proved too much of a challenge for them. I thought I might lose Jamie after his parents returned but he was well settled with me and it was an easy commute from my home to his job in London. I hoped Fiona did not mind that her son chose to remain living at my home. I knew she missed him terribly. Still, in a small way I was glad to be returning the favour of her months of dedicated care for me and Sally. Fiona knew I would always look out for her "boy" and that he had a home with me for as long as he wanted. Sally's career was flourishing and she was being offered lead parts in cabarets and shows in Europe and more exotic Far Eastern locations in Singapore and China. What a girl, just like her dad, charismatic and talented, but happily, much more grounded and sensible. I was sorry that her and Jamie's romantic relationship was over. That would have been the perfect way to cement the two families that had come through so much trauma and drama together. Fiona and I had got as far as fantasising about the beautiful grandchildren we would have if they married. They remained good friends, which helped when Sally came home from her trips abroad. No awkward atmospheres to negotiate around.

Three months after Ricky's funeral, the police contacted me to tell me that Guy had recovered consciousness but that he seemed to be suffering from amnesia and was in a psychiatric hospital for the foreseeable future. Unless his memory returned, he would be unlikely to face charges. Frankly, I did not care if he never recovered his memory - or went to jail. He was out of my life for good and my joy and gratitude for just being alive was growing stronger by the day. Sally was right, blonds do have more fun.

*

The warmth of the July sun caressed my back as I sunbathed in my secluded garden. It was Saturday and I'd had a busy week at work. I figured I deserved to relax with the weekend papers. I was almost dozing off when the phone hand set buzzed from under my sun lounger. *Typical*, I thought, glad I brought it outside with me.

'Hello?' I said, hoping it wouldn't be Aunt Doreen who loved to share all the family news with me. It would take ages. We were a large family.

Silence.

Breathing?

'Hello? Anyone there? I can't hear you.'

Had the sun gone behind a cloud? My back was cold. I saw the date on the Weekend Review section of my paper, July 4th.

ABOUT THE AUTHOR

Pat Abercromby published her debut fictional novel in 2017. For several years she was a free-lance journalist and has always enjoyed writing. Life had other plans, leading her down unexpected and challenging pathways. It was in her early seventies that Pat finally had the opportunity to write her first novel.

Pat has had an eclectic and changing career pathway which included medical research, in the UK and Germany. A successful career running her own medical sales recruitment business followed until two babies came along in quick succession. A recession in the mid-seventies, a move to Singapore with her husband (a long-haul flight engineer flying big jets) was the start of a sixteen year odyssey of living in Germany, Saudi Arabia, and America. Working as a radio broadcaster and freelance journalist whilst living in Saudi Arabia, Pat wrote extensively for the Arab News, Saudi Gazette and in-flight magazine for Saudi Arabian Airlines.

Her return to the UK saw another career change when she retrained in massage and body-work disciplines gaining a Post Graduate degree in education. She set up a training school with her business partner Davina Thomson and for over a decade, taught Seated Acupressure Therapy courses throughout the UK and Ireland.

In 2007 Pat's husband suffered a devastating stroke. She gave up her successful career to become his full-time carer. Eight years later, her husband safely in residential nursing care, Pat had the opportunity to pursue her interest in creative writing which led to the publication of her first novel 'Just One Life'.

Pat has two daughters, three grandchildren and lives in Buckinghamshire.

BIBLIOGRAPHY

1980-1986: Arab News, Saudi Gazette, Ahlan Wasahlan In Flight Magazine, feature articles

2000: Seated Acupressure Massage, Corpus Publishing

2002: Seated Acupressure Therapy, Corpus Publishing

2017: Just One Life, Clink Street Publishing

2018: The Knife Edge, Amazon Kindle and paperback

p.abercromby99@gmail.com

Phone number: 07970 669112

13329020R00098

Printed in Great Britain
by Amazon